MOMAYA
ANNUAL REVIEW
2011

A Momaya Press Publication

London, U.K. & Gaylordsville, Connecticut, U.S.A

First published in the United States of America, 2011 by Momaya
Press. The moral right of Momaya Press has been asserted.

Printed and bound in the United States

ISBN 978-0615540665

Table of Contents

* Honorable Mention
** Published under the theme "Greed"

List of Illustrations

Foreword

Welcome to the 8th edition of the Momaya Annual Review.

The common experience of writing is a solitary affair. Whether they are actually alone in their home or sitting in a public space, writers throw their words into the void of computer screens and notebooks. Most writers rarely experience the pleasure of seeing their words in print, and more rarely still, hear from their readers.

Maya and I founded Momaya Press to redress this balance. We provide a forum for writers to get feedback on their writing through our website, and we sponsor an annual awards ceremony where writers get to hear their works read aloud by actors and meet the judges who selected their work for publication.

We encourage the audience to try their hand at writing their own stories. Momaya Press is building a community of readers and writers around the world, to inspire people to express themselves and to support each other.

Most of our waking hours are spent doing things that are functional. It's a celebration of life to take time out to write a piece of fiction that exists for no purpose other than as an expression. It is our own unique, individual, never-to-be-replicated contribution to the world in which we live. A piece of writing can change how we perceive the world. By changing how we think, we then change how we live our lives. Through our individual contributions, we can collectively shape the world we all experience every day – we hope for the better

Greed

Greed is theme for the Momaya Annual Review 2011. In the First Place story, "Where There is a Will", greed is illustrated quite literally when a wealthy man dies and friends and relatives scramble to discover who will inherit. Greed for power is shown in our Second Place story "Mao Yanshou" exerts his position by casting off a beautiful would-be bride for the emperor. Greed for sexual experience and freedom from the constraints of marriage are explored in the Third Place story "Will You Miss Me?" In all of these stories, the greedy learn their lessons. Perhaps our readers will learn the same lessons vicariously – and live their own lives a bit more virtuously as a result.

Every year Momaya Press chooses a different theme. Having run eight story competitions, we have noted how the theme can dramatically affect what type of stories people submit. *Greed* seems to have elicited more stories that impart a moral lesson than the 2010 *family* theme, or the 2009 *alienation* theme. No one submitted a story than implied that greed was good.

Sincere thanks to the judges who reserve time in their busy schedules to read the entries, the actors who perform the winning stories at our annual awards ceremony, and most of all our readers. Our judging panel included Andy Callus (Copy Editor,

Reuters), Kay Peddle (Editor, Random House), Polly Courtney (five time published novelist: Golden Handcuffs, Poles Apart, The Day I Died, The Fame Factor and Defying Gravity), and Alice Shepherd (Assistant Editor, Penguin).

Encouraging your contributions

We hope that this collection of stories inspires you to submit your story to our competition. Our 2,500 word limit is about five pages typed — it's something you can write during your lunch break, instead of watching TV after dinner, or by getting up a bit earlier on the weekend. Submit your story to Momaya Press and someone who doesn't know you (that is — not your mom!) will read your story, will reflect upon it, and make a considered judgement on whether your story should be published in this year's annual review. It's an incredible validation of your ability. It's a thing of beauty to share your vision with the world.

We thank the many readers and writers who have supported Momaya Press over the past seven years, and we encourage everyone who reads these words to submit their short story to our competition. The theme for 2012 is "Heat" and we are accepting entries on our website until 30th April 2012.

Respectfully yours,

Maya Cointreau and Monisha Saldanha
Directors
Momaya Press
www.momayapress.com

Undertone

Christian Cook

Anya's final sweep of the bow was as if she had delivered the coup de grâce in a sword duel. The last note reverberated around the empty theatre until only the white noise from the speakers remained, lapping back in like a gentle wave.

It was probably the most beautiful rendition I had heard her perform, but there was no applause; there was only silence.

I flicked my eyes across to Malcolm, the theatre director, but his gaze was transfixed on a particular seat. Even Anya, rigid and breathless with the violin at her side, was staring at that same seat.

Apart from the three of us from the theatre, the only others present were Ewan and his assistant, Zak, a pair of experts Malcolm had hired to investigate the issue. Milling around the aisles, they were interchangeable; they both spoke like presenters on a science show, but were dressed like students. Their eyes, along with all their equipment and cameras, were also focused on seat C3.

Anya was standing in the middle of the stage, as she felt

uneasy about venturing into the darkness of the orchestra pit. Malcolm and I were sitting on the steps at opposite sides of the stage like bookends.

"Anya, can you give me the last two bars again?" asked Ewan.

The violin filled the hall once more and then fell silent.

Now even my eyes were on that same seat, occasionally straining at the tiny displays on the various motion sensors and infrared cameras dotted about to see if anything flickered in response to an unseen presence.

Above the ambient hum, I heard Malcolm's inhaler puff into life to extinguish the rasping edges of his breathing. The scenery on the stage was doing little to calm his nerves; a hellish backdrop from a production of *Don Giovanni* loomed over us. Most of the lights were also switched off so as to limit any interference being picked up on the array of twitching gadgets.

"Cold spot over here," announced Zak. "Anything under the floor, Vic?"

I sifted through plans and blueprints. My actual job was sound technician, but I knew enough to serve my purpose as a general technical reference.

"Every inch has got some sort of piping, wiring, or secret tunnel under it," I answered, tracing my finger over the industrial spaghetti in front of me.

"What's in that exact spot?" asked Ewan.

"It's near a pipe. Water pipe."

"How near?"

"Within two or three feet."

"Well is it two or is it three?"

Armed with the map, I hopped down onto the floor and walked the route of the pipe right through Zak's cold spot.

I returned to my perch on the steps. Zak tapped the instrument in his hand, and then exchanged this for another, which looked to be an ion detector.

"Are you getting anything up there?" Ewan asked vaguely at the stage.

Malcolm's eyes darted about nervously.

"I felt something," announced Anya softly.

"What do we still have running?" asked Ewan.

I sighed. "Heating's off, most lights are off, air con's off. Just a few lights and the sound system."

"Can we lock it all down?" asked Ewan.

"And stand in here, in the dark?" I queried.

"We have candles," he answered.

"What about the sprinklers?"

"It's an old system," said Malcolm. "Not that sensitive. Probably needs replacing."

"Anya, will the violin be audible without the amps?" asked Ewan.

"For the whole place or just to there?" she asked.

"Just to C3 will do."

"It should be okay."

She turned to me for my opinion.

"We can try it," I said, shrugging.

I set about powering down the sound equipment while the two of them unpacked some very large cathedral-style candles. They constructed a circle of them around Anya.

"Do I have to have this around me?" she asked.

"It will help you see," said Zak.

"And be seen," added Ewan.

"It just feels a bit weird," she said.

"It does look... ritualistic," I agreed.

"They know what they're doing," said Malcolm. "Anya will be okay in there, won't she?"

"Relax, everyone," said Ewan. "This is not some freaky ceremony, it's science. But, remember, even if *we* are focused on the seat, *his* focus will be on the stage."

"I don't mind, really," said Anya. "But leave a gap, so I don't burn my arse if I need to go pee."

Once a few candles were lit, I switched off the last of the lights. There were candles encircling Anya, a row along the front of the stage and a line up each aisle. Ewan spent some time fussing over the location of the candle nearest seat C3, as he wanted to keep it visible, but not have too much light and heat affecting the infrared readings.

"Are we clear now?" asked Ewan.

"There's still your electronics throwing out all manner of waves and signals," I said.

"It's all calibrated," he said, turning away from me.

I thought my scoffing at this was inaudible, but Anya fired me a look in response.

"Anya, whenever you're ready," announced Ewan.

"The same piece again?" she asked, shrugging with the violin and bow in each hand.

Ewan paused. "Can we try something else... something... maybe a little less... "Go-ey'?"

"Go-ey?" queried Anya.

"Slower, more sombre. Anything like that."

"Anything but..." muttered Malcolm.

"Don't worry, Malcolm," she replied. "Anything but..."

Anything but *Der Doppelganger* by Schubert is what they meant. Every other seat in the building has been replaced and refurbished several times, but C3 is a shabby antique with a faded 'RESERVED' label across it.

That last time that seat was occupied was also the last time that song was performed here.

In 1914, a wealthy doctor, Henry Lockyer, was sentenced to be hanged for the brutal murder of his young wife. Though he was unable to use his status to escape punishment, he managed to persuade a judge to allow him a final visit to the opera. Chained between two guards, he listened to the entire evening in silence.

When the show concluded, he slumped over in his chair. His death was listed as natural causes though no proper explanation was ever forthcoming.

It was believed that he had died quite early on and so had missed hearing most of his last opera. Some even speculated that he had not heard a single note.

The performance that evening was Schubert's *Schwanengesang*; many were convinced the melancholy theme of lost love, even if just read on the brochure, was enough for the doctor to suffer a fatally broken heart.

Later reports of strange chills, or a lone man seen sitting in the theatre, started the rumour that Dr. Henry Lockyer was revisiting the theatre in order to hear the music he had been denied that night.

The shrewd theatre owner, Fred Swayne, saw an opportunity to cash in on the story and promptly slapped the 'RESERVED' label onto the seat.

Paranoid that if all the songs from that night were played again then the ghost would depart in peace, Swayne trawled through the play lists of every performance and rehearsal to identify which of Schubert's *Schwanengesang* had not been repeated.

From the remaining songs available, he selected *Der Doppelganger* and immediately banned it from being played within the theatre again. And every subsequent director since has religiously upheld the rule and that song has never been played in the building since.

Malcolm was certainly a believer. He had given Ewan strict instructions that he was looking for proof of a presence, but did not want Dr. Lockyer removed or harmed in any way.

Malcolm had already rung up a huge bill with Ewan and Zak. They had sat during an entire evening show and recorded nothing of note and then spent a long night with just Malcolm where they achieved very little other than to leave the director a nervous wreck. It was then that Malcolm had hit upon the idea of bringing in a musician after hours to encourage Dr. Lockyer to make himself known.

Anya was one of the finest musicians on our books and I was

shocked that Malcolm had even asked her, let alone that she actually agreed to do this. She concluded another piece and silence resumed. With the sound system off, there was no white noise to punctuate the void; a vacuum of nothingness swallowed the room and it felt as if my heart was beating inside my skull.

The flickering candles threw overlapping shadows onto the walls that danced in the silence. This caused all our eyes to nervously glance about to check on any movement about us. Ewan extinguished a few of the wicks as he moved about, deciding that they were interfering with his readings. A few candles were moved more into the open or tucked behind seating depending on the angle of nearby cameras and other devices.

"Can we try a different tune?" shouted Ewan. There was a frustration in his voice that suggested the current no show was Anya's fault and I was not going to bite my tongue if that suggestion became vocal.

Anya sighed.

"I should have brought my flute," suggested Malcolm, trying to soften the atmosphere. "I could have given you a hand."

"You play?" asked Anya.

"Nothing to your standard. And don't really have the lungs for it." He tapped the inhaler in his jacket pocket.

"You'll have to play for me one day," she said.

"Ironically, I forced myself to learn *that tune* at home," he said, not even wanting to name it.

"Really? That's a tricky one, especially not on the piano."

"Yes, I know. I usually use the vocal part for the tune."

"Difficult B minor."

He waved for her to keep quiet and not say any more, as if just mentioning the key would invoke one of them to begin whistling the tune.

"Malcolm, don't worry, it's just a key."

"I know, I know, but still, let's leave it there."

"In your own time," said Ewan from the aisles below.

There was a slight stamp from Anya's foot; she looked exhausted.

"Let's take a break," I suggested.

"Best not break the flow," said Zak.

"I need a coffee," I announced, stretching my arms and ignoring him. "Anyone else?"

"The machine's out," said Anya.

I checked my watch. 2:10 AM. I slumped back onto the steps.

"I need to visit the ladies anyway," she said.

"You want me to come with you?" I offered as she passed.

"I don't think you need to," she said, smiling.

"No, no, I mean... not right in. Just..."

"It's okay, I know. Thank you." She lowered her voice. "There's nothing here that can harm me."

"I thought you said you felt something?" I whispered back.

"I did," she said with a mischievous grin. "Cold... and a bit silly."

I did my best to hide my smile as she left, as Malcolm was glaring in our direction. He had been firing me looks all night. I was not sure if these were just self-conscious glances or glares to ensure I was keeping in line.

It's not that we don't see eye-to-eye; it's more that we both recognise that we are different species. Malcolm says that I have a closed, technical brain and he has an open, creative mind. And he always uses those same words; I have a brain, whereas he has a mind.

Debating the need for these ghost hunters earlier, I had said, "I just like to be black and white about issues."

"I'd rather not live in a world without colour," he replied.

"Malcolm, a computer can still display the Mona Lisa on its screen, but, behind the scenes, it just sees 1s or 0s."

"No one should live in a world of just 1s and 0s when there are Gs and 5s and Ws and curly brackets and semi-colons."

"Binary can still involve all the other letters and more, but when you boil it to down, it's a clear cut case of a 1 or a 0; yes or a no; on or off; black or white."

"You're too fond of always 'boiling things down." You should stand back and learn to appreciate the whole. If I take you for a beer at lunch, will you appreciate the pint as a whole or will you attempt to boil that down, too?"

I have to admit that I had no comeback to that.

"I think we need to create the feel of an audience," announced Zak, bursting through my recollection.

I rechecked my watch, but kept silent.

"We could put some programmes on a few chairs," suggest Malcolm.

"Hey, Malcolm, go and sit in C2 or C4," suggested Ewan.

The director needed to sit down rapidly and suck hard on his inhaler.

"C6 will do it," offered Ewan. "Even C10 might be close enough."

"Vic?" said Malcolm, looking imploringly at me.

"No, not Vic," said Ewan. "No disrespect, but I'd like to keep any negativity at a healthy distance."

I was obviously not calibrated correctly; wrong polarity for his sham science.

"We could try some EVP," suggested Zak.

This is what they tried the other night when they gave Malcolm nightmares. *'Electronic voice phenomena'* involves recording questions onto a sound recorder and then leaving a gap for a spectral presence to reply. Upon playback, these experts insist you hear the dead speaking. The reality is that the sensitivity of the microphone is up so high that the silence forces the machine to amplify background noise just to find any audible sound. This roaring hiss gets bent into words by people wanting to hear a voice.

It's very much like finding pictures in clouds.

I was happy for them to wander about with their naïve DIY tools, misinterpreting basic background temperature changes and magnetic signals, but I was not prepared to stay and listen to them trample clumsily all over my acoustic knowledge.

"Could we just try with the music one more time?" asked Malcolm, hearing a door swing open.

Anya returned and gave me a conspiratorial smile.

Because she was so serious about her music, I had always assumed that she was a cold person. The mischievous humour I had seen was causing me to step back and see a different Anya.

"Okay, Anya, can we try something a little more in keeping with the atmosphere?" asked Ewan.

In keeping with what atmosphere? Was the ghost of the doctor visiting here in order to listen to spooky tunes? With the candles and the sombre music, it felt like they were trying to make an atmosphere rather than discover one.

Anya poised herself to begin playing again. Even though she was just wearing jeans and a sweater, and sporting a practical ponytail, she looked quite a haunting presence herself in the candlelight.

She launched into an incredible version of Chopin's *Funeral March* and I had to drop my head to hide the huge smile on my face.

Ewan and Zak said nothing, but their stances and faces made it clear that they were not impressed.

Anya responded by morphing smoothly into John Williams' *Imperial March*, the Darth Vader theme from Star Wars.

She stopped and looked over at Malcolm. "Malcolm, I'm tired and it's been a long night. We're all tired."

He nodded slowly. "I know."

"If Dr. Lockyer really is going to come out for a tune then there's only one that he's waiting for and he's never going to hear it, is he?"

Malcolm's silence signaled that the night was over. The silence continued as we all packed up our belongings and left the building.

Outside, I found myself standing alone with Anya.

"Sleep at last," I said.

"I am not sure I can sleep now," she said.

"Not spooked, are you?"

She laughed. "Only by those two. No, I just feel like I've gone past sleep."

"I do have some coffee at my place. It's not far."

She smiled.

"Sorry, that must've sounded a bit cheap."

She collapsed against me for support and nestled into my arm. "I am happy with your cheap coffee."

* * *

I was awoken midmorning by the phone. It took me a while to find my bearings and the caller hung up as I answered. I dialed the number back and it turned out to be one of the cleaning staff.

When they had told me all I needed to hear, I went back into the bedroom where Anya was just beginning to stir. I gently woke her up and told her to get dressed quickly, as we were needed back at the theatre.

The fire was not as bad as I had envisioned. A few rows of seating were damaged and a lot of the carpet was now just ash; the flames had reached the stage steps, but had finally been dowsed by the sprinklers before they had taken hold.

One of the firemen told me where the fire had started, but I didn't need telling; I had already guessed.

"I left some sheet music here," muttered Anya, slapping her

forehead.

"Are you them that were playing last night?" asked one of the cleaners, hovering nearby.

"Yes," I said.

"You left more than your music. You left one of your instruments on the stage, too."

"You had your violin, didn't you?" I asked, looking back at Anya.

She nodded.

"Didn't touch it or pick it up," continued the cleaner. "Whenever we do, we just get into trouble, so I left it up there."

The flute was in two pieces where it had been dropped. Anya walked up the steps, saw it, and rushed backstage calling Malcolm's name.

I lifted up the two parts and slotted the flute back together again. I found my eyes fixed back on that charred seat as I heard his name fading into the labyrinth of passages offstage.

And then there was silence; I heard his name no more.

Like Marny

Somer Brodribb

Marny watched Dora, her eight-year-old, eating breakfast: spooning up cereal, swinging her feet, twisting her pajama top in her hand. Dora used to twist her hair, especially the bit behind her ears. Not anymore. Marny'd had it cut short. Dora looked like a bird, some dodo with stray feathers on its head. Except she wasn't stupid, she was a little swot.

Marny said, "Your hair's gone all sticking up on your head; it's too wiry isn't it; I bet you wish you had fine, straight hair like mine."

"No," said Dora.

Marny's face froze.

Dora said, "I want to grow it back."

"What about what I want?" retorted Marny.

Henry had just spent £48 on a smart red children's doctor's bag, complete with surgical cap, gloves, mask, bandages, spatula and a stethoscope Dora wore everywhere. She was wearing it now. Marny was not going out to work so Dora could have affectations and a college fund when she was just going to do the same with her life as Marny had done, and why shouldn't she, why shouldn't she want to be like Marny. Not every child is meant to be a doctor and the sooner Henry got that in his head the better for everyone, Dora included.

"You're disgusting," said Marny. "Look, you've got jam on the spoon and it'll be on your face next. It makes me sick just looking at you."

"Where?" asked Dora.

"On the spoon, now it's on your face, you'll be a laughing stock going to school like that," said Marny.

Dora wiped at her cheek with her sleeve and looked to Marny to see if that got it off. Marny shrugged and got up and poured herself more coffee.

Henry came in the room. He bent down and squeezed Dora.

"How's my baby girl?"

"Hi Dad."

He went to the fridge. "No more cream then?"

"I don't need cream in the fridge, do I, when I've got my weight," said Marny.

"Any milk?" He lifted the carton that was beside Dora, and it shook empty.

"Little greedy guts has taken all the milk," said Marny.

"Sorry Daddy, I can pour some for you." Dora held up her cereal bowl to tip out some milk.

"No honey, that won't work," said Henry.

He went to the cupboard and stared inside. "Any evaporated?"

"This isn't Tesco's Express. I work full time." She didn't want to, but he kept saying they needed the money for Dora.

"Okay," Henry said and pulled out his blackberry.

Marny watched Dora get up and go over to the utensils drawer. Dora pulled out a large colander, then got a stool and went to the cupboard and took down a mug; she put the colander on top of it and started draining off milk from the cereal. Marny watched it tip over and splatter milk and cereal all over the floor. She jumped up and grabbed Dora's hand and slapped it hard. Dora's mouth opened in shock, she didn't cry but her face got red.

"I don't have time to clean up after you all day," Marny said, "I've got to leave for work soon."

Henry put his phone in his jacket. "Dora, go get ready for school." He didn't look at Marny, but said: "I'll take her today." Dora turned and ran out of the kitchen.

"Get back in here," Marny shouted down the hall. Then she turned to Henry. "I'm not her maid. She can bloody well clean it up."
"I just thought it would be easier if she wasn't in your way for a bit, it's not the end of the world, Marny. Lighten up."

Dora had not returned.

"Dora," Marny yelled. "What did I say?"

Dora slunk round the door, and back into the kitchen. "Well come on, clean it up!" said Marny.

Dora reached for the dishcloth.

"Not the bloody dishcloth! You idiot," said Marny.

"She's a child, Marny."

"You always defend her, Miss Do No Wrong. Nothing's too

good for your little Dora."

Dora reached for the paper towel and started to unravel it.

"Don't use too much, we're not made of money," said Marny.

Dora wound the extra back on the roll and pulled off one single square section of towel. Marny sat back down and watched Dora kneel down and splash the bit of towel about in the Cheerios and milk but there was too much liquid, so Dora got up and took the sopping handful over to the sink to wring it out, dripping milk along the floor in a trail.

Marny jumped up like a shot and snatched the towel out of Dora's hands. "Just get out, you're useless, get out of my sight." Dora left. Marny unwound a wad of towels until she had a baton like candy floss in her hand and then threw it down over the puddle. She went to the cupboard and pulled out a mop and pushed the towel around with that.

Marny knew Henry watched her go over the dry space with several more swipes and a bit of muscle, she knew he was waiting for an opening.

"I'm going to be late as it is," he said, "I can drop her off."

"No," said Marny, wiping her forehead with the back of her hand. "I'll do it."

Dora appeared back in the kitchen, rushing, ready. "I'm ready now, I can go with Daddy." She must have heard.

Marny said, "No, you're not ready. I want your bed made before you leave."

Dora turned pink, 'But I'm ready, I've got my books and I'm ready now!"

"No, I said."

"Right then," said Henry, leaving.

* * *

Marny backed the Ford Fiesta out of the driveway. She had things on her mind. Marny wanted a family holiday; she deserved one. She started to think about her holiday: it would be in Egypt, in Sharm el Sheik, and it would be all inclusive. Marny could see herself on the balcony overlooking the sea and sand, and she would lie there on the beach in the sun and young men would bring her drinks. She would wear a new bathing suit that hugged smooth against her taught middle. She would wear a lot of gold jewelry at the beach, or maybe not, maybe scarves. She would go to all the buffets, and the drinks would be all free and fancy and she would know their names and tell the other tourists what to order; she would recommend. There would be live entertainment, and she would lie on her lounger and bask. People would ask her where she got her bathing suit and where else she went for holidays.

Marny slammed the brakes down just in time not to hit the pedestrian on the crosswalk. The car slapped to a stop and they both pitched forward and back.

"Mom, my stomach hurts," said Dora.

Marny turned and peered at her. Dora was leaning forward, holding her stomach. Then she put her fingers on her wrist, she seemed to be taking her own pulse. It was all an act to get attention.

"It's because of the way you gulped down all that milk," Marny said.

Marny reared the Ford Fiesta to a halt at the school entrance.

She said, "Call your father to come pick you up. With all that commotion this morning, I didn't have a chance to tell him I can't do it today. I've got my refresher course until 6 tonight and I won't have a moment to myself all day."

She spoke while looking in the rearview mirror, watching the traffic she could pull into as soon as Dora got out.

"There's nothing in the fridge and the delivery doesn't come till 8. So don't think tea will be ready and waiting on the table for you."

"Dad always makes it anyway," said Dora, already well outside the car and holding the door at arms length. Marny turned to say something just as the door shut. Through the glass she could see Dora climb resolutely up the stairs and into the school. There wasn't a safe opening into the rushing stream of cars but it was her turn and their brakes; she swerved into the traffic.

Yes, Marny absolutely had to go on this trip. Then she could tell her sister all about it, the schoolteacher with a nice, fat pension and a Head of school husband. Marny would tell Cathy what a wonderful time she had, and how the food was great, and that she saw the pyramids and it was all lovely. Cathy couldn't go anywhere as she was always trying to get pregnant and was afraid of getting some stomach bug. Marny imagined Cathy spending every weekend looking at a timer with her ass in the air and chuckled to herself. That was one thing Marny had that Cathy didn't. A kid. Marny had half a mind to wish one on her.

* * *

She pulled into the parking lot. Same church hall every year.
First day of the three-day annual refresher to keep up her Health
and Safety certificate and get a break from the office. Marny liked
being the designated Health and Safety person at her job and
knowing the rules about what could and could not be done. Her
mother had wanted Marny to be a nurse but frankly she never
could stand the thought of mopping up after people. So, she'd
dated the assistant manager of the local Ford plant. He was long
gone now but she'd been there ever since he got her the job. She
hadn't asked him for one but went along with it because she
expected to quit when they got married. That didn't happen; he
stepped out and away on her, married some cast off mother of two
from Birmingham and even moved there, and Marny had to keep
working. Why he'd wanted used goods and someone else's brats
and not Marny she'd never know. The woman must have had
money. Anyway she'd never let that happen again, so she got
pregnant on purpose with Henry, the new manager at the satellite
plant, and he'd married her.

Now Henry liked Dora and wanted her to have the best of
everything and still Marny worked.

She walked into the church hall. The course was in the main
room, same as her old slimming class. She was late but she knew
the drill. She really didn't need this requalification. She could
teach it herself, she'd been so often. She found a seat and dozed
through the first hour, counting the moments until the cigarette
break.

Suddenly, the instructor finished his explanations and started dividing people into groups of three for practice demonstrations using their kit. Marny was teamed up with a bloke from the fire department; he was gorgeous, he must work out a lot. He had veins bulging up and coursing like rivers along his hard, thick arm muscles. The other was a woman from social housing, probably a lesbian by the way she dressed. Not that Marny knew anything about weird shit like that, but she could tell. This had to be one. Marny looked at the fireman and rolled her eyes, like look what we've got stuck with.

He looked down at the mats; she followed his gaze. The mats were clean and blue, they must have cost somebody some money. The woman was a real know-it-all, she wanted to go first, and the hot fireman offered to be the patient with a cut to his palm. These two got down on the mats, he held his hand like it was bleeding and the woman got down on her knees beside him. Marny didn't bend down; she could see fine standing over them. The woman squeezed his hand and elevated it, laid him down, and took out a long bandage. She placed the end with the sterile cotton pad on the wound. Then she placed another roll of bandage in the palm and told him to grip with a closed fist and wrapped the remaining length of gauze around, making a real production out of it. She'd left the thumb out.

Marny said, "You don't do it like that." She said it loud enough so the instructor would overhear, he was walking by and stopped.

"You left his thumb out," Marny repeated.

The instructor squatted down and clasped his hands together and observed. He was wearing an expensive watch, how much did he make a year?

"Actually, you need to do that to see if it is turning blue," he said. "It's a great way to see if the bandage is too tight."

He watched the woman finish the treatment, wrapping another long length of bandage close around the hand. He looked up at Marny and said, "Now, what would you do if you are first on the scene and you see someone lying on the ground and their leg is bleeding?"

She said, "I would check for a pulse."

"No, the first thing," queried the instructor. Marny glared, crossed her arms and looked away. She refused to be drawn.

At the break, the woman from social housing and the fireman were talking and drinking coffee beside the stacked chairs and the woman was rubbing her neck. They were getting along like a house on fire, Marny thought to herself. The fireman was young, hot, and he liked the dyke better than her. Marny hated their guts. This morning she hadn't had time to fix her hair and do her make-up; she hadn't realized this was going to be a beauty contest. He was too short anyway. Why were they letting these runts into the fire department? He would probably kill to be as tall as she was. That's probably what his problem was. She out-classed him in the height department by a mile.

* * *

Maybe now Henry would finally see that Dora wasn't a perfect little princess.

"It's time to call the police," Henry said. That changed things.

"Why?" said Marny. She checked the clock on the microwave.

"It's just 7. We should wait."

"Are you kidding me? I should have called when I got home. I shouldn't have let you stop me. We've just wasted time calling around to her friends and the school. I'm calling 999."

Henry picked up the phone from the hub and started punching the numbers. His hand was shaking.

"Give me that," Marny snatched the phone out of his hand, "It's not 999. It's 101 for things like this. You'll cram up the lines."

"What?" said Henry.

Marny paused. "Are they going to want a reward or something, do you think? They're going to want some money, aren't they."

Henry held onto the kitchen chair. "I don't know," he said. He looked confused.

"I think we should wait a little longer."

"For the love of God Marny, you call or I will."

Marny tightened her grip on the phone, and then poked the on button. She locked eyes with Henry.

"Hello, this is Mrs. Smith." She put her hand over the phone and said, "They want our address."

Henry nodded and she gave it to them. She cleared her throat. 'The thing is my husband forgot to pick up our daughter today . . . 8 she's 8 . . . from school yes . . . 3:15 they get out . . . I did call the school . . . they said she missed the afternoon . . . I did call her friends, they said she'd been sick in the loo but I don't know about that."

Marny's voice rose with indignation. "Of course we've searched the house." She said loudly to Henry, "They think we're stupid."

She put the phone back to her ear. "How would I know where she could have gone?"

She turned again to Henry, "Honestly, who do they get to answer these calls . . ."

Henry was facing the hallway, his face changed. Marny watched relief and love and light flood into it. He became young. Dora stumbled into the kitchen, half asleep and blinking. She was wearing that bloody stethoscope. Henry rushed over and picked her up.

"Oh my God, my God," he stroked Dora's hair.

Marny said, "Never mind," and hung up.

"Where were you darling. Are you all right? I looked in your bedroom. Where were you?" said Henry.

Marny watched them both. Henry held Dora on his waist with both arms underneath her; she had her arms around his neck. "I fell asleep in the little room." Dora said. She started twisting his tie.

Marny wasn't going to let her get away with that. She said, "Your daughter has started sleeping in the cupboard, didn't you know that?"

They just looked at her, two pairs of dark brown eyes that didn't respond, eyes she couldn't see into.

"Dr. Dora Hubbard, sleeps in her cupboard," Marny sang. She bent forward sharply, pointing her face at theirs. 'Tell that to your patients, Dr Dora: "Please attend my surgery, in a cupboard",", she mimicked.

"It *is* my surgery," said Dora. 'My doctor's bag is in there." Marny crossed her arms and watched Dora grip her stethoscope with one hand and her father with the other. Held up by Henry, Dora was almost eye-to-eye with her. She'd be a teenager soon. There would be boys. That would be the end of this *Everything for Dora* nonsense.

"You know what? I've changed my mind. You can have your hair as long as you like."

The Red Shoes

Sharda Dean

There they were. The red shoes. He kept passing them on the way to work, and there they were on the way home again. Winking at him, flirting with him, so shiny and feminine. They would look utterly fabulous on a ballerina's exquisite feet. Walking into the shop, he immediately felt too big and cumbersome, everything here was perfectly poised, perfectly balanced, rows of glass shelves, perfectly polished, gleaming quietly. There was no guarantee they would fit, but he did not have any choice, these weren't the sort of shoes you could hesitate over. He didn't want to ask the price; that would be common somehow. After all price did not matter when purchasing something so beautiful. So he tried to be calm and to appear in control, decisive "I'll take these in a size 8 please".

"Yes sir, let me check."

She was gone awhile and he stood there, trying not to look awkward, but obviously looking exactly that. He looked at the shoes a little more closely, not daring to touch. Some pairs looked as though they were suspended in midair. He imagined reaching out to touch them and then the whole row toppling like dominos.

She came back, the pretty young girl and opened the box for him, he looked quickly, and said "yes, that's fine" and she swept past him to the counter. He followed, taking out his wallet and wondering which of his many credit cards would look most impressive. He knew Agnes would love these shoes, and although she would not look as good in them as she would want to, they would thrill her.

Walking back to the train station he felt slightly self-conscious holding the smart bag from the shoe shop. It looked decidedly feminine and did not sit well with his sharp business suit and Oswald Boteng shirt and tie. He had cultivated a certain image at work and the bag did not seem to blend with that. He hoped no one from work was in the same carriage.

It was hot and sweaty on the underground and there were no seats anywhere, so he had to negotiate holding on to the bar with the bag constantly being nudged by other people's feet. No one had any class anymore. Agnes did, but she was about the only one. He saw a young lady wearing leggings and a pair of Ug boots with a sloppy batwing t-shirt hanging off one of her shoulders, chewing gum. No class. Agnes would never wear something like that. It wouldn't suit her either, but even if it did, she still wouldn't wear it. Her icons were more sophisticated, Sophia Lauren, Ingrid Bergman, Catherine Deneuve, Jackie 'O'. Real women, with tits and an arse you could grab; each buttock and breast more than a handful. He smiled. But there were so few of those around now, it was all coke-head pop stars or anorexic footballers' wives. They all wore designer clothes and still managed to look like sluts.

When he arrived at the station car park, his head was full of Agnes. The thought of the shoes made him feel excited and all the office politics melted away. He wanted to know how they would look on her, he couldn't wait to get home.

Once inside his house, he could breathe more freely. Everything here was calm, orderly. The sleek lines of his kitchen caressed his eyes, the marriage of dark, warm, Indian rubber wood and brushed stainless steel worked well. The paintings so painstakingly chosen were also painstakingly lit, pride of place in the lounge was a John Sargent, often on loan to various galleries. The silky sheen of the paint echoed in the fabrics of the two low sofas.

He carefully prepared supper, trying to put all thoughts of the shoes out of his head, Bach's Goldberg variations in the background. He deliberately took time cooking, then laid the table meticulously, opening a smooth Pinot Noire, pan frying a tuna steak and plating it carefully with a fresh rocket salad dressed with homemade virgin olive oil and lemon juice. He couldn't abide shop bought dressings, how lazy could you be not to put some salt, pepper, mustard, garlic, oil and lemon juice in a jar and shake it?

When two glasses of wine had been consumed and the juices of his meal soaked up with a thin slice of hand baked bread, he went upstairs, taking the bag with him. He called her name softly as he climbed the stairs, slightly drunk but 'none the worse for wear'. Agnes, Agnes, oh how I missed you. He opened one side of his wardrobe, hanging up his tie and suit. He put his cufflinks away in the carved wooden box. Then he took off his shirt and slid off his pants. Agnes, where are you? He opened the other side of his wardrobe and surveyed Agnes' array of evening dresses. He would really have to buy her something more normal to wear, some sort of Miss Moneypenny outfit. Pencil skirt and silky blouse maybe. The thought of the necessary purchase sent a frisson through him.

He picked out a long red dress. Spaghetti straps, v-neck, ruched over the bosom, with the skirt delicately pleated in chiffon. He remembered the shop he bought it from in New Bond Street, so perfect, everything to die for. It was Agnes' favourite place, her spiritual home.

He opened his bottom draw and looked at the neatly folded sets of lingerie, some still wrapped in tissue paper. He smiled, how like Agnes, so fastidious. He took out a very tasteful red set and put it on, inserting 'chicken fillets' along the way. 'Not bad' he thought as he admired his cleavage in the full length mirror. The French knickers were very flattering, very feminine and with his newly waxed chest and arms he felt delicious as he slipped the dress over his head and it washed over his body as spiritually cleansing as any holy water. Here she was. Agnes turned to the shoe box and opened it, gasping with delight, her heart pounding. He would be so upset to have to return them. Would they fit? She slipped her feet in, yes, they were fine. A little tight, but with a bit of wearing in... She loved the slippery feel of the shoes on the thick pile carpet.

Next, jewelry of course, no outfit could be complete without it. Now, with so much red, Agnes would have to be careful not to choose anything too tarty. Too much red could send the wrong message. What would Sophia do? What would Audrey do? Simple yet elegant, always simple and elegant. He opened the other box on his dressing table. He spritzed on some Issey Miyake parfum and applied some concealer around the eyes. He should really have shaved but she couldn't wait to see herself all dressed up. Some foundation next, eye liner, mascara and lipstick. Eye shadow maybe, but no, she hadn't mastered that yet, and it made her look too 'dinner lady'. Reaching up to the top of her wardrobe she removed a chestnut wig and ceremoniously placed it over his very short hair. It was cut very softly, very flattering, and changed the shape of his face immediately, giving it undeniable felinity. When she saw the total effect in the mirror she was struck dumb. She could feel a lump in her throat. She was everything he'd hoped she would be. She'd been waiting for this moment every since he first saw those shoes in the shop window. She knew this outfit would work. Even the delicate diamond necklace was perfect. She felt delicious, excited, full of life and imagined she was dancing with someone, someone who would treat her like a lady.

When he woke up the next morning, he still had the dress and shoes on. He slipped them off and put them away carefully. He turned on the radio to catch the overnight events in the NY and Tokyo markets and switched on Bloomberg TV on the flat screen panel in the bathroom while he shaved. Another day, another dollar, but it was worth it. To buy is to live. To buy well is to live well. To buy perfectly is to live, perfectly.

When he got out at the station and walked to work, he passed the shoe shop once more. The red shoes in the window had gone. In their place was the most stunning pair of cream and white stilettos. He stopped to look more closely. Yes, they were perfect, and he knew just what to wear them with.

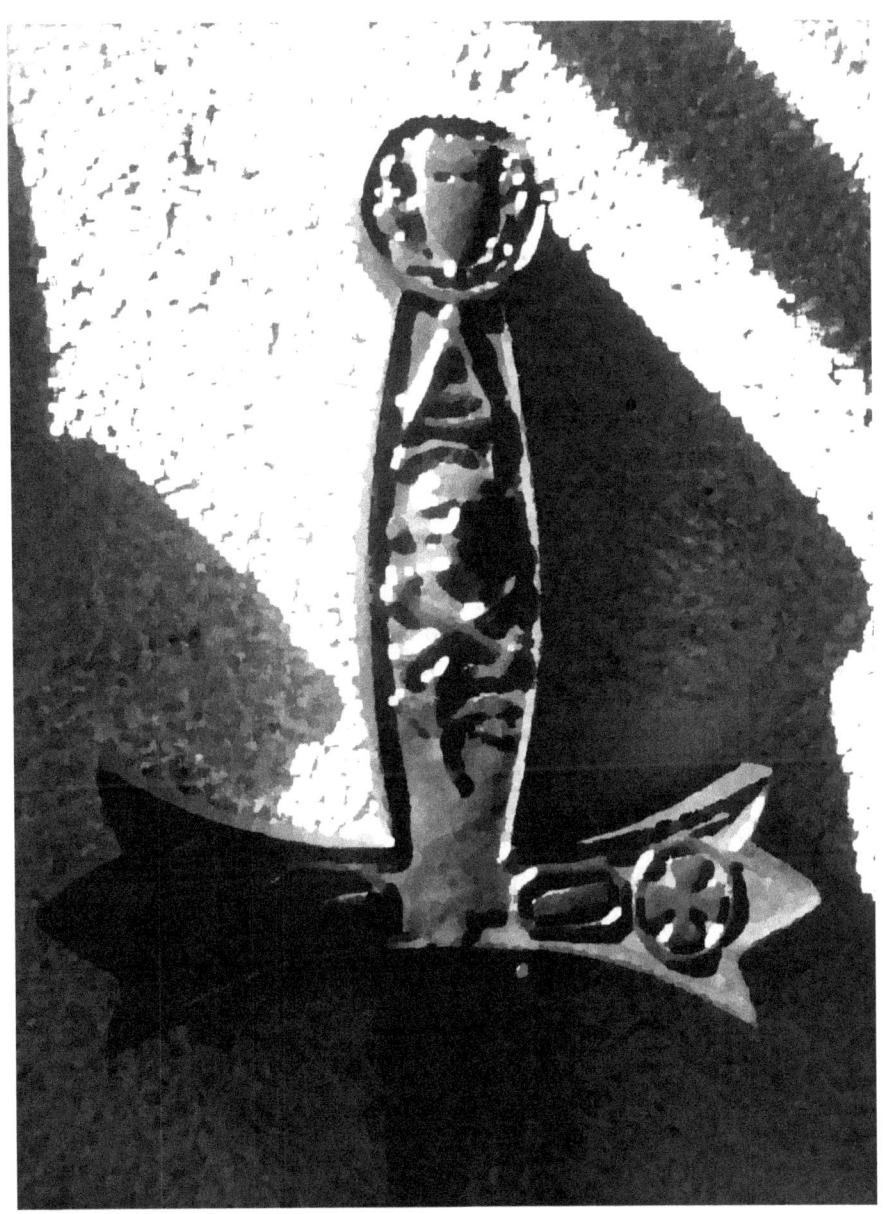

The Good Sin

Suzanne Gaskell

"Mum, quick, there's something coming up the road."

Mrs. Maisie Day let the fly screen door slam shut behind her as she rushed outside to see what her daughter was screaming about. You couldn't afford to miss any excitement when you lived under the limitless blue skies, on the isolated edge of the great deserts of Western Australia.

Violet Day pointed down the melting strip of bitumen that was the main road into town and there shimmering in the heat haze, was a small convoy of trucks.

Maisie wiped sweat from her face with a tea towel and swatted at the flies that were desperate to nest in her eyes and counted six colourful trucks all towing large white caravans and she smiled.

"Well, Violet Day, you're about to see a travelling show."

Maisie and Violet watched the trucks turn off the main road outside of town and followed their slow progress over the unsealed track towards the bore well by the sand filled dust that lifted and settled in the breezeless air.

The town they lived in was a petrol stop for travellers. Along with petrol, passersby usually bought an ice cream cone or a bag of chips to break the monotony as they drove in their air-conditioned cars to places Violet could only dream about. It was the local cattle station owners and their hands that kept the little outpost of pub and general store alive.

The town's nearest neighbour was a multinational mining operation a hundred kilometres to the north. The company had built tiny, tin roofed houses for their workers, along with a pool, a small outdoor movie theatre, a store and a grog shop. They hadn't set up schools or community centres because families distracted the men, so only a few of the grimmest of women stayed in the barren compound.

That evening something miraculous happened. The small patch of black desert surrounding the bore well blossomed into a thousand coloured lights and gaudy music blared from tinny speakers, carrying for miles through the cold desert air.

Tray trucks and Utes spilled out freshly washed bodies dressed in sun stiffened clean clothes. Some men came on horseback, bashing the dust from their hats onto their thighs as they dropped to the ground. A few aboriginal families, camped far out in the desert, walked in, their children's eyes large as saucers at the fairyland that had miraculously grown up out of the primeval desert floor.

There were fairy floss and toffee apples to be bought and rides that spun you fast or wobbled you up and down and booths where a rifle shot or the throw of a dart could win you a large stuffed animal with shiny black plastic eyes. In the dazzle of coloured lights, strong men gagged as they watched a clown swallow the blade of a sword, while young isolated men nudged each other and giggled as an attractive girl performed a Polynesian fire dance. Jugglers moved among the crowd and magicians pulled glinting dollars from behind unsuspecting ears and the music thrilled on and on.

Three tents had been erected and two were filled with glowing lights.

"Come up, come up," cried men in bright suits. "For only one shiny dollar you'll see the wonders of the world, brought to you at great expense from distant countries far too remote to even name." Men and a few women paid their dollar and disappeared inside the small tents only to return happy or embarrassed at the show they'd seen. The more curious poked their heads into the third tent but it remained dark and silent.

Suddenly the music stopped!

The rides, even the fairy floss machine fell silent as a tall thin man climbed slowly onto a dais. The crowd started booing but the man stood still and waited for them to quieten and when he spoke it was with a voice so soft, they had to lean forward in order to hear him.

"Friends, they call me Nachash and I know you all wonder about the empty tent. The tent will be used on our last evening in your fine town; in two night's time. In this tent there will be no feats of strength or throwing of knives, neither will there be dancing girls or magic acts. What will happen in there is something so extraordinary; it will change your lives forever. I am going to sell you whatever you desire."

"You don't know what I desire," yelled a young man from the crowd. Men offered him a few suggestions and the crowd roared with laughter.

The man on the dais raised one long thin arm to still the noise. "Remember, nothing is free, you will pay if you want what I offer." Then he was gone, disappearing into the crowd as quickly as he'd appeared and within a moment's breath the music and the rides restarted and people were laughing and trying their skill, the intrusion forgotten.

The next evening the travelling show was as busy as the night before; it didn't matter that the acts, like the fairy floss were exactly the same. For a few hours, this tiny glittering bubble under the immense black dome of the great southern sky was a salvation that allowed these lean and sunburnt people to forget the loneliness and hardship of their lives.

The tall stranger did not appear again!

On the last night, the coloured lights danced and the music was gay but the crowds pouring in were subdued, not interested in the gaudy entertainment of the previous evenings. They stood in small groups talking quietly, glancing now and again towards the lonely, darkened tent. When the tent's lights went on they started shuffling uncertainly towards the opened flap. The tent was empty except for a small stage at one end and a few bare globes dangling precariously, scattering dark shadows around the walls.

The crowd moved in silently and then the tent flap was closed from the outside. There were no seats and the air quickly became hot and stale with the crush of bodies as the tall thin man stepped onto the dais. Nachash was dressed in an old fashioned black suit and his dark hair was oiled and shiny.

The man looked at the upturned faces and pointed a long bony finger towards the back of the room. "You, over there," his voice thundered, and the whole room started with the shock of its power. "The other evening you told me I didn't know what you wanted, am I correct?" The slight young man nodded, embarrassed to have been remembered. "Come forward," ordered the voice. The men in front parted, allowing the chosen one to stand before the stage.

Nachash studied the young man carefully. "I could say it is height you crave, to be as big and tall as these men around you but that is not it." Nachash stood very still, his small dark eyes narrow and glittering on the boy. "Yes, that's it. You covet hair. You are tired of having to wear your hat wherever you go to hide your baldness. People think you rude when you enter their homes with your hat on because they don't understand you're humiliation, do they my son? You'd do anything for a full head of hair."

The young man instinctively put his hand on his hat when Nachash mentioned baldness and now strong hands grabbed at him until his hat was wrenched from his head. The boy had suffered from alopecia for most of his life and his head was entirely bald except for a few mangy tufts that sprouted sporadically over his pate.

"Give him back his hat," roared Nachash, his tongue flicking spittle at the crowd. Do you think I will stand for this sort of degradation?" and his audience recoiled before him.

The boy scurried away and the tent became quiet, waiting for Nachash to speak and although his voice was soft now, it captured and held them fast.

"People have told you there are seven deadly sins but I say they lie. There are six sins that will carry you to damnation, but Greed is not one of them." He felt the crowd stiffen. "Greed my friends, is given to us on the wings of angels for our betterment but there are those who wish to keep the secret of Greed to themselves."

Nachash nodded his long, thin head towards a girl who had magically appeared on stage and the sound of a distant drum throbbed through the tent. "Behold, Cleopatra, Queen of the Nile, lover of Caesar and Antony, ruler of the great lands of the Pharaohs. Do you think it just ambition that earned this young girl her fame? No," cried Nachash, "She was filled with greed, greed for position, greed for land and greed for love. Without greed, Cleopatra as we know her would not have existed."

"Just what are you trying to sell us Mr. Nachash?" A voice yelled from the crowd.

Nachash smiled. "Firstly, I am just Nachash and my business is selling Greed. It is Greed that will make you as famous as Cleopatra, or if you wish, as rich as Louis X1V." He lifted his fleshless hand and pointed towards a man lounging on the stage in a long wig, a satin coat and silk stockings.

"Louise X1V, envied by all other kings for the opulence of his palace of Versailles, the same palace that shines so brightly, even unto today. People called him, 'The Sun King,' and no one dared challenge his authority as king or as God's representative, here on earth. His riches, like his love life were enviable and all this from a boy who was thrust into kingship at the tender age of five. Do you think this child could have survived the machinations of a French court and a civil war if he hadn't used Greed to keep a firm hold on his kingdom? I think not."

Nachash reached for a glass of water on a small table at the side of the stage and waited for the question he knew would come.

"The only problem mate, is that Greed can't be bought because it's a feeling."

Nachash returned his glass to the table and placing his hand over his heart, replied, "But my good man, I have Greed for sale," and he watched as his audience glanced around trying to find barrels or boxes that may in fact hold Greed.

It occurred to some of the hard bitten men in the tent that this stranger might be trying to con them and their voices became loud with questions and insults. Nachash let their voices rise with the pounding drum until finally he put up his hands in a call for silence.

"Do you all agree that Love is a feeling and when it is taken away from you there is only pain and emptiness?" Many in the crowd nodded. "Over the centuries man has been taught that Greed is a sin, therefore we have lost the ability to feel Greed the way we still feel Love. Trust me when I tell you that the natural feeling for Greed is as strong as the natural feeling for love but the devil understood the power of avarice and took it from us by using guilt as his weapon.

Look at the people today in your cities and your communities who have ignored the devil's teachings. Millionaires and billionaires, mining magnates, news barons, the C.E.O's of international companies, star athletes, writers, super models all know that Greed is not evil. Remember, Greed doesn't always mean riches; it can be anything you covet above all else. One person may covet ruling his own country, while another may covet being the spiritual leader of that very same country. Then there's Greed for knowledge, a wonder that has brought humanity out of the dark ages, think of computers, aeroplanes and medical cures. Greed is good for us all as individuals and as a society."

It was a woman's small voice that broke the reverie and the big men in front turned to hear her. "The church says that greed is evil," she said modestly. Nachash smiled gently at the little lady then swung around and pointed sharply to a young woman who appeared in a blaze of light.

"Joan of Arc!" and his voice rattled the tent walls. "A young girl, burned at the stake by priests for having divine discourse with God. His instructions were to reclaim her lands from the English and this teenage maid obeyed and broke the siege of Orleans. If this is true, and you may read the story for yourselves, God himself used Joan as an instrument of greed as He bade her win back the lands of France.

Is it not reasonable my dear lady that if we all got what we wanted as God intended us to, the priests of all religions would lose their power over us and go back to Satan where they belong? If you look towards the most prosperous countries, are they not also the greediest and the least religious? Can you not see they are the ones most blessed by God?"

"I have said enough, it is time for you to buy from me or not." Nachash reached into his pocket and pulled out a large black velvet bag with a silver pull string at the top. "Those who choose to buy should come up onto the stage, one at a time. In this bag I have small crystals that will absorb as much greed as you wish to pay for. The more money you spend, the greedier you will be.

When you hold the crystal in your hand you will feel its power immediately, but if you say you do not feel the power, it will mean one of two things. Firstly, you have not purchased enough greed to accomplish what you covet and you will need to buy more and secondly, if you do not feel the power, it means that you are an unworthy person who was never meant to achieve anything on this earth. If this is the case, I will refund your money in front of everyone, so all will know I am not a charlatan.

Now as you come forward breath strongly and feel the power of greed surge through you."

All through the night the calls went up. "I feel it Doug, do you feel it?"

"Sure, I can feel it comin' right up from me feet, how about you Johnno?"

"Wow, boys, I'm quittin' me job tomorrow and headin' for the big smoke. I just got this feelin' there's somethin' waitin' for me there, somethin' big."

"I'm comin' with you Johnno."

"And I'm comin' too."

It was almost dawn when the last person departed clutching his crystal in his hand and wondering if he wanted to own his very own country or have a date with the blonde barmaid at The Grand Hotel, in Perth

Violet Day woke early that morning, anxious to wave goodbye to the departing Travelling Show. She walked down the road towards the bore well, but she hadn't gone very far before she realized the site was empty. There was no rubbish, no holes where the tent poles had been driven into the hard rocky ground and no tyre tracks; it was as though the whole camp had never existed.

Violet turned to go home but quickly stopped and stood absolutely still as she watched a long dark shadow slither towards her. The snake coiled its body and then raised its head and bared its fangs.

Maisie Day was cooking breakfast when Violet came in the backdoor.

"They've gone mum, not a sign of them anywhere."

"Those travellers move pretty quickly love, they've got a lot of territory to cover if they want to get to the next town before nightfall, besides they'd be used to packing up fast."

"But I didn't even hear them drive through town mum; you'd think I'd have heard that."

"Well, I suspect you're tired with all the excitement and all, never mind, they may come back this way again." But neither Maisie nor Violet believed that.

"Vi, I'm going to buy meself one of them prospecting machines that beep when it hits metal; there's gold out there and I've got a feeling I'm going to be lucky."

"Greedy, more like it," said Violet, as she bit into the first of her four buttery, toasted bacon and egg sandwiches ".

Maisie stared at her daughter. "Violet Day, I hope that's not a snake you've brought into the house?"

"Oh, he's okay Mum, I found him near the bore well."

"Well, I trust he's not poisonous Vi, I don't want to be calling the Flying Doctor because you got snake bite and get it out of the fruit bowl while you're at it.

"Don't worry mum, he's harmless," and Violet Day picked up Nachash and took a bite out of the apple he'd curled himself around and headed for her bedroom.

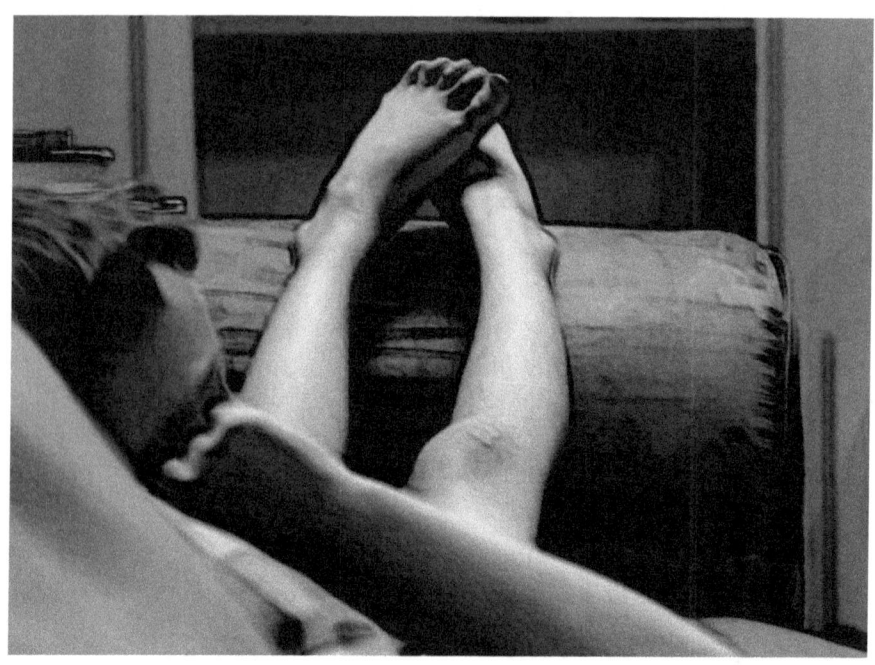

Reading in Bed

Vivian Hassan-Lambert

Get up you fat arse, I can't help myself thinking when I look at the stranger sleeping beside me. It's so hot, even with the window open my body and the sheets are drenched with sweat, and then there is that familiar sour smell emanating from between my legs. Next to me, my companion's wide back is erupting in a series of red peaks, the kind that teenagers get. On the brown carpet near the bathroom door lays an empty bottle of Johnny Walker and a crumpled packet of Marlboro Lights. His back is so white and soft I want to kiss it.

Why oh why dear one did you do it again after you promised yourself and Carol that you wouldn't?

You're a slut, a whore, that's why.

Yesterday, the brain lying beside me now zeroed in on me from across the bar room floor – his brown corduroy jacket hanging attractively open and his ball belly pressed against an ironed cotton shirt, the posh kind you'd buy at Harvey Nichols. He moved so fast his group of book-friends, adoring students, didn't know what hit them. He looks a bit like Philip Seymour Hoffman only cuter, blue eyes, slightly pink around the edges and adorable white lashes. How could I resist?

My leg against his – like two ethnicities – one brown, one white. I'm thin where he's fat. I'm firm where he's soft – my body still tanned from all that naked summer swimming at the Heath. It's easy to press myself against him, curve my hips around his, tuck my arm under his and tickle that land of soft skin beneath his neck.

He turns quickly, eyes still closed – smacking his lips like a granny about to speak – and takes my nipple in his word-smith mouth. I curve upwards like a sphinx, creating pressure where our groins meet and he groans, eyes still closed, and I feel him getting hard beside me.

After we're done I roll off, our bodies covered in soapy slime. I have a headache and my mouth is dry. He clicks his tongue, eyes still closed, and throws his arm out missing my head by a few centimetres. I sit up – no classes today or tomorrow, we're on study leave. His clothes from last night are laid neatly across the desk chair. My black tights, skirt and halter top are splayed in a trail on the floor between the bed and front door.

Two weeks to the deadline.

Two weeks to come up with the goods and get myself out of this job.

On the table under the mirror he's left his keys, phone and bulging black wallet. I can see his rolled up dissertation – the one he said last night was 'shit hot' – poking out from the corduroy's deep pocket. I smooth a few plastered hairs away from his forehead and he turns and begins to snore like a cat asleep. I make my way to the desk.

The wallet is almost grey with cracks, it's the kind my Dad used to have and it's stuffed so thick it can hardly fold. There's a picture of a woman inside, the kind of snap people take at school then give to a sweetheart when they are about to leave. Her tidy brown hair is held back with an old-fashioned Alice band, she's neat but she isn't smiling.

There are tons of receipts, coupons, business cards and a small piece of newspaper, carefully cut and folded, advertising scrap metal for an industrial project. I look back at my lump asleep on the bed, is he a scrap-heap entrepreneur? There's not enough money to take, only a tenner, no credit cards either, just two loyalty cards and a worn out old ha'penny, for good luck I suppose.

I look in the mirror above the desk – there I am, hair a mess, sacs under my twenty-five-year-old eyes, make up smeared – barmaid about to get promoted I hope.

He stirs a little, then flips his arm back onto my empty pillow, exposing a tuft of soft red hair. I can smell him from here – fresh sweat, alcohol and cigarettes. I push open another window, it squeaks but the Professor doesn't move.

His chino pockets are little better than the jacket's – an unopened condom, a gold ring, a rubber dummy. He didn't say anything about a wife and children, but then why would he? He's got a small plastic covered notebook with scribbles so tiny they're hard to read. *She moves like the night,* I manage to make out. *Check out second monologue. See Fred about Tuesday.* A half eaten pack of Tunes, more cigarettes.

He knows the art of giving pleasure – last night he must have licked every inch of me, explored every orifice, made me moan until I felt I was being turned inside out. Carol, my psychologist – *I pay her enough each week* – says that I'm looking for my father, that I need to get used to living on my own, love myself before anyone else will love me. But I live on my own don't I? Do I cook stir-fry with a partner beside me? Do I curl up in front of the Hollyoaks omnibus sharing the Times Supplement on Sundays? Do I carefully plan for retirement or a slew of children? I'm not interested in relationships: I'm interested in me, I'm interested in getting out of this shit-hole job, of passing through the portal of subservience and into something better.

Yes, I've had boyfriends, for a week, a month, six months.

Like Richard, last year, poor chap – three thousand miles away from home – he thought I was a princess, wanted to take me back to meet the parents, and I almost did, almost bought the wedding-dress dream. He was an academic, like this lump – guess I'm attracted to brains – but in the end I couldn't do it. When I told him the deal was up he cried and shipped stateside. Now he's an advisor for Chase Manhattan and he's discovered he's gay.

Red-top turns again, smiling. When I met him last night we talked across the mahogany counter and he said he liked my mind, he said I was sharp and quick, then he bragged about his PhD dissertation. *Top secret,* he slurred after three Margaritas and a bottle of Chardonnay. Didn't want me to say a thing, afraid his colleagues would up and steal his work, *plagiarism* he called it.

There's something rotten about Red-top, like a discarded apple on a rotting rubbish heap. Something familiar also that I could get attached to, but then, of course, there's that ring in his pocket.

It's eleven a.m. and light splays through the horse chestnuts outside. There's a crack of thunder and it's started to rain again. Do I close the window or let the sill get wet? I go for the latter as it's too hot and I don't want to suffocate. In an hour I'll have to go to work at Lorenzo's Grill – wipe down table tops, shine up the bar, load the fridge and chalk up the board. My university assignment's due in two weeks and I can't get my head around it – five thousand words or I don't pass and without the pass the new job's not mine. Red-top doesn't ask, so I don't tell him – they hardly ever do – he won't stay around long enough to find out.

His chest is broad and hairless and punctuated with pale pink nipples – one kiss and then a shower. Even in sleep his lips grin; I press my mouth against his, my rear pointing skywards. Without eyes opening, he kisses me back, tongue filling my throat, penis lying gently like a spent balloon. I pull away, brushing my breasts against his face and he clips the air with his teeth – like an Egyptian suckling grapes.

My hair is dripping wet now and smells like cheap shampoo; my legs criss-crossed on the unwashed sheets; I turn the page. He yawns and opens his lovely blue eyes. He peers up at me like a boy adoring his mother and pulls at my arm. I flick him away annoyed.

"I'm reading in bed," I say. This dissertation's good; I could use it, I grab a pen and pad from the desk and begin to write.

I Have Learned to Breathe Underwater

Jon Flieger

I have learned to breathe underwater

But I still float, which is a problem.

My solution is to drive my car off a bridge and see if that helps. The car will sink and since I'm very good about always buckling up, I will sink too. It will hold me down and I'll have a comfortable place to sit as I breathe water.

The world is built inside the skeleton of a whale and I will sink down among her bones. It's all fairly straightforward.

The problem with my solution is that when you drive a car off a bridge they don't leave you among the bones and Coke cans of the riverbed.

People try to rescue you. Which is nice, when you think about it, but counterproductive to my project.

Coke cans browning from red oxidized despite less oxygen

richness in water and I never really understood that and he pulls me from the car.

Struggles towards the surface clutching. Goodbye cans. Goodbye whale. Goodbye car, and that of course is another issue. I have a limited supply of car and after approximately one attempt to breathe underwater I should run out. Approximately being an uncertain word and certainly you could ask why I would use it. Why does anyone do anything and "Oh God" and panting breaking surface "Oh God." He pulls us to the riverbank, he's on top of me before I can move.

"Breathe! Miss can you hear me? Breathe." He pushes at my tits like that's where breath comes from. Bends his neck and spits air into my mouth. "Breathe."

Yeah. I am.

"Oh," and he looks down at me, his eyes red from the water. His hands are bloody from clawing at my car door, forcing it open. Ragged skinned raw hands that are, I should mention, still on my breasts.

Oh, I say, too. Hi.

"Hi," he says, confused and then realizes that his hands exist. Sits back on his heels and blushes. I sit up. I wipe him from my mouth with the back of my hand. Cough but otherwise breathe evenly. He is gasping and sputtering.

"Are you okay?" pant pant pant he has little tears running from his eyes but that is maybe river water. "I saw you go off and I, I just dove in, I" he's dumping adrenaline now and gulps air through his throat. He is almost certainly going to throw up. "I thought you were, that you were going to" and he throws up down the bank. Sirens in the distance.

People on the bridge pointing at us. Oh motherfuck it.

You feel okay now? I ask him after a few heaves.

"Better. Yeah. Are you? Are you okay?"

I'm good.

I get to my feet, tug down my shirt. He's pushed my bra up so that I'm wearing it as a necklace and when he turns to vomit some more I try to adjust myself, cold and clinging wet.

The sirens are closer now. That's a conversation with the police I don't particularly want to have. I'm breathing normally and looking down at him. We should go.

"Wow," he says, struggling to his feet to stand next to me on the bank.

"You're a tough lady."

He's too young to say lady anything but ironically and I suppose I can respect irony from someone who is half-drowned.

C'mon. Let's go dry off. I turn and begin climbing the dirty sandmud of the bank. I can't see what he does behind me but I imagine he wears a puzzled expression and shrugs. A moment later I hear him begin to climb behind me.

His name is Matt and we sit together on a bench in the park. People give us strange looks because we are sopping wet and men try to look at my nipples through my shirt without looking like they're looking at my nipples through my shirt. A young couple walks by and as they pass the woman begins to whisper angrily at the man. He looks down and keeps looking down until they are out of sight. A puddle spreads outward from our bench but the sun is warm and we will dry.

His name is Matt and he says "Are you sure you don't want to, like, give a statement or something?"

A statement.

"Yeah. Like, to the police or something. I don't really know how these things work but as I understand it.um.statements happen? Are involved somehow?"

That is not how I understand it at all, I tell him, but he doesn't laugh. He chews his lip. He looks down and then quickly looks back up. Inadvertent guilt I think, but can't be certain.

If they fish the car out or whatever they do they'll see who it belongs to and they'll call me. I can talk to them then.

"Okay," but he doesn't sound reassured. Which is fine. Chews his lip. As his hair dries it's a scruffy midlength and lighter than I first thought it was. He hasn't shaved today. Or yesterday most likely. I can see his nipples through his t-shirt. He is concerned about a woman he just met because in meeting her, he pulled her from an underwater car wreck. He would probably be a nice man if I didn't have to sit here and talk to him.

Nothing talks underwater. Whales and dolphins click at each other, I guess, but that is approximate language. There aren't many dolphins near this river in any case, so it isn't a concern, if

I'm speaking to geographical relevance. But Matt asks me what my name is and my name is Beth.

"Beth, you seem fairly calm about nearly drowning."

Oh, I say.

"Oh," he says. And chews his lip as I look on.

I tell him I can breathe underwater and this time he laughs.

He is a nice man. I consider asking to borrow his car so I can drive it into the river, but he'd probably let me do it without suspecting and I would feel bad. Also I would have to ask him. And that is probably more talking than I want to do.

We all come from the water. We just walked up onto Africa or whatever looking for food. But nothing lasts forever, I just want to go back.

Don't fool yourself, this isn't infinite. I can breathe underwater and I can go back.

He doesn't even own a car, I later learn. He was riding his bike when he saw my car go over. It was stolen while he was pulling me out of my sunken car. His bike and my car both gone, oxidizing to brown, which is fine, but he was upset. Why does anyone do anything.

I read that bull sharks can travel through fresh water. The females are larger than the males and they can traverse rivers, even jump up rapids like salmon to find better food sources. I wasn't down in the river long very long so perhaps I'm looking at an insufficient sample size, but I didn't see any bull sharks. I could sit at the bottom of the river and wait to see a shark. To have them see me. I could try attaching some weights to myself and jumping in, but then I guess I'd have to carry the weights with me all the way down to the river. I should have tried that first, when I still had a car to carry the weights down in. I'll have to carry them now, and the chains to attach them or whatever I can find.

That seems like a lot of trouble.

Matt walks with me around the park. I wish he wouldn't, but he jumped off a bridge for me and got his bike stolen so I feel kind of obligated to not just ditch him. He'd be confused. He thinks he saved my life.

He doesn't know what to talk about so he asks me what I do for a living and I laugh at him. He asks my last name.

de Rivière, I tell him. Beth de Rivière.

"Oh, that's pretty."

It's also not true.

"What?"

It doesn't matter. Just call me Beth.

"Oh."

Oh.

And we're quiet for a short time. The squirrels and robins and vultures in trees sleep and the park is quiet, too. Animals crawl through bushes while there is sun for them and children eat plants and shards of glass as their parents doze.

Bull sharks can swim in fresh water, I tell him. If they want to. He does not look at me but he smiles. The sun has dried us but the inside of my shoes still squish. We smell of river. He says, "The blue whale is the biggest creature in the world and it's the biggest
creature that has ever been, um. In the world. Bigger even than dinosaurs. And, like, water dinosaurs. Plesiosaurs."

Plesiosaurs?

"Plesiosauruses? Plesiosauri? Loch Ness Monsters. You know, fatty paddlers, but with snake necks. The blue whale is bigger than any of them."

Oh.

And I'm glad he told me that. I wonder if he knows the world is build inside the skeleton of a whale, but I don't ask him.

At home in the tub I sink down and hold myself under the water. From below, I watch the ceiling of my bathroom like I expect something of it. Read patterns and faces in the tile.

It's not the same as the river, but it's okay.

Breathe. Breathe.

He called me lady. It's too bad about his bike.

I was on the news tonight. Or my car was. My phone rings a couple of times but if it's the police they don't seem too upset. Nothing screams out of my answering machine. I stay underwater. I gave Matt my number but told him he wasn't allowed to call me for a few days and that the first thing he said to me couldn't be "are you okay?" These instructions seem simple enough, I don't imagine it's him calling. But who knows. How are you? Are you okay? Let's talk about our jobs and our families and every horrible thing we've ever thought about. Let's talk forever and use every word we've ever heard like they mean something. Just like they mean something. I breathe more water and another call goes to the machine.

Matt has taken me out a couple of times. Or we've met somewhere because we don't have cars, but we have been in locations together. He drinks beer and doesn't like what I drink. He works for a bank or an office or something and doesn't like that either. He speaks in acronyms and pretends he doesn't notice that I don't listen to some of the things he says.

We went to bed together once but he had a lot to drink and nothing much happened. He was upset about it. I didn't care and he was upset about that, too. He thinks he saved my life.

Some cultures believe that if you save someone's life, you're responsible for it. For everything they do after. So if I kill, like, a few people. Probably that's your fault.

"Maybe try not to kill a few people?" He laughs. Of course, if I cure bone cancer or such he probably gets to take credit for that, too. Probably he shouldn't hold his breath waiting.

At the pool at the Y I have to surface regularly. Pretend to gasp needy for air. Otherwise a lifeguard will come arcing through the air at me, pull me shoulder skin rubbing off onto the deck and press his mouth to mine. What an interesting way to meet people I have discovered. If I was interested in meeting people. I should make use of it, though. Write an article for Cosmo. But then Matt would be responsible for the drowning of lonely people. He has enough to worry about.

It doesn't bother me.

"Well it fuckin should."

You're too drunk, it's not a big deal. It doesn't matter.

"What the hell does that mean?"

What does anything mean? And this said dismissively to hurt him and I'll admit that. He leaves shortly after.

His apartment has a shower, not a bathtub. I tell him I don't want to stay at his place and that upsets him, too. A shower stall is a urinal for the skin and I have little use for urinals. It's not about cleaning, it's about breathing. I don't explain this to him. He gets upset when I talk about breathing water.

"I don't understand why you'd want to kill yourself," he says, and then he sulks. And that part is okay because we are quiet for a time. But it's not a good quiet for him, and it's not an underwater quiet for me, so it's only okay. It isn't infinite. This isn't infinite. He shouldn't fool himself. I shouldn't. I can go back to Africa. I can breathe underwater. He doesn't even have a bike anymore.

The phone rings and I don't pick up. Sounds are different underwater. I say my name into bubbles and I know what I'm saying, but no one else would. Matt would make a joke. The fluidity of language? Something like that. His jokes are mainly terrible but I like them anyway.

Bubbles again where Beth should be. I remember the river.

They're doing construction on the bridge and I know that. That's why I'm driving there. The rails are down and there's only tape up along the side of the span, so I don't feel bad driving through it. I don't want to ruin anyone's work, this isn't about that. The car goes over, I imagine the wheels windmilling like cartoon legs without purchase in the air. To be honest, I expect weightlessness. I expected a forever moment from childhood. Jumping off a swing at the apex of arc and terror and joy and hanging there for days before But no. The car noses into water like into brick and I surge against the airbag. I'm good about buckling up and I wasn't driving fast and it's a low bridge but I hit the airbag pretty hard anyway. Between the material of the bag obscuring my vision and being dazed, I do not see the water creep at me across the hood of the car. This is disappointing. The car begins to levels out as water fills its lungs, its spaces and crevices. I'm relieved the car levels as it sinks, and I won't be looking straight down at the nothing of river bottom. The bumper driven like a stake into the riverbed.

The water rises to my chin. I dip my head and begin to breathe. It isn't the same as drinking, but this is a gulping nonetheless. A gasping as the water covers my eyes. I can see.

The water is dark and in no way pure but I can see.

What do the fish think of me? I don't see any fish. I see some tires and browning Coke cans, and somewhere behind me are the supports of the bridge. I can't see any fish but they're here somewhere. Bull sharks who will puzzle wordlessly about my life. I see the whale bones of the river's foundation.

I sit and breathe I gulp and see. I say words into bubbles and they travel out around me. They will find dolphins who will click bubbles back at me or they won't. It doesn't matter. I have learned to breathe underwater. I will wait for bull sharks. I will see what they see.

I see a man cut into the water, swim with desperation towards the car cradling me. As he attacks the resistant car door I see he hasn't shaved today. He grabs me, stabs fingers at the catch of my seatbelt. Pulls me upward.

No. No not yet.

You didn't save me, Matt. This said not to hurt him, but why does anyone do anything? It may have been to hurt him. I didn't want you to save me.

He looks hard at me for a second. Gets up and picks his jacket up off my floor.

"Why don't you go fuck yourself, Beth?"

Yeah. Why don't I just do that. And he looks at me again but this look is sad. He has shaved today. Probably because he knew he would see me.

He shrugs into his jacket.

"You can give me a call if you want, Beth. I'm done calling you for a while."

Okay.

"Okay."

But my phone rings that night and I don't know if it's him. I sputter bubbles and slog sopping from the bath to the phone but whoever it is hangs up before I get there. I return to the bathtub. Say words into bubbles but forget what they were when they were in my mouth.

The Logic of the Mine

Sarah Hegarty

I see it in my dreams; it frames my days and nights: the maw of the mine, gaping like a wound in the burnt remains of the forest. You might think the location God-given, if you believed in the god these people do. When the mine has finished with a man only the crooked-beaks will find him.

Daylight is pushing through the mist when I slip out of Mackenzie's office. No one sees me join the line of workers heading towards the cages. Cold, damp earth clings to my feet, and I stay close to the man in front. He has made himself shoes from wideleaf and twine. The detail, his effort, makes me laugh. He must be new. He thinks he can find a way to exist here. But already the string is coming loose. I raise my foot to stand on the flapping leaf and finish the job. But maybe I'll let him find out for himself. That good deed will bring me luck, on my last day here.

Around us, shifting strands of white hang over blackened stumps. The mist disguises movement and sound. But as we near the mine, the creak of the winch and the yells of the overseers seep through. And under that, a low murmuring – the kind of noise that passes for singing down there. There must be one less mouth; one less pair of hands.

The last miner to die was Lieno. He was near the end of his time; took one chance too many. Mackenzie called him out at food break, and without warning one of his men put his knife to Lieno's gut. The miner's skinny body crumpled, his blood spurting in the dust. Then the guard bent over the dying man, finished the job and reached into the wound. He held up the bloodied treasure for us all to see. I heard the sound of vomiting.

"Just a reminder, gentlemen," Mackenzie said. "Now back to work."

* * *

At the entrance I wait while the man with the wideleaf shoes is searched. Sure enough, under his tongue – an amateur! – Mackenzie finds a folded prophylactic from the whore house.

"Planning to use it?" he says, waving it in the man's face. He stretches it over one of his thick fingers. "Easy to swallow, eh?"

The man tries to run, but in a movement which seems too swift for his bulk Mackenzie trips him, handcuffs him as he lies on the ground, and calls the guards. When they come over he throws them the limp piece of rubber.

"Make it worth his while," he says, as the guy is hauled to his feet and dragged away.

I step forward.

"Lucas!" Mackenzie greets me with a slap on my back, his belly bumping my hip. "Another twenty-four hours, eh? No slacking just because it's your last day."

His breath stinks of beer. By the end of the day he'll be slumped on his chair. He grins his wide, toothless grin, sweat beading his forehead. He doesn't know how I find the gems, and he doesn't ask; he sees only the tally under my name at the site office – year in, year out, the most productive worker. Mackenzie and I understand each other, even if he goes too far sometimes.

He waves me through, towards the cages.

The throaty sound of an engine pierces the mist. Out of the corner of my eye I see a truck approaching, along the access road from the interior. It looks different from the lorry that brought me here. But things change, in twenty years. It's not carrying prisoners, so must be bringing equipment. It stops at the gates. On the back is a large, oblong box. It's the wrong shape for a coffin: and they don't usually bother with those.

There's the clank of rusting metal and the cage appears at the cliff edge. We are herded in, and the gate locked: too many have tried to jump. The freedom to choose your own death is a privilege. Each cage holds fifty men, but there are more of us here. Even at this hour we smell of sweat, and dirt: the dribbling taps outside the dormitories are no use against the dust that stains us, inside and out. No one speaks. I feel hot breath on my skin. The cage swings out, out, over the mine. >From here, the workers in the pit base are smaller than the biting insects that invade the dormitory at night.

I'll miss none of this.

At the bottom the cage stops, and thuds into the wall. The overseer grabs an upright bar, unlocks the door and lets us out. The empty cage rattles back up.

I pick my way between sluggish bodies of men who have spent the night here, in the icy chill that falls after sunset. Voices call out to me, whether in warning or greeting I can't tell. Those who are able leave the pit at dusk, on the rope ladders lowered for us. The ladders are wound on large rusting handles. You can imagine the fight to climb on. Some men are dashed against the walls as they are dragged upwards; some are pushed off, and left in the dirt until the following day.

But I can easily grasp the wavering rope. So each evening I return to the sleeping quarters, my wages under my tongue, the soft skin feeling each ridge, each edge and jagged point. I don't remove it until I'm away from the mine. Often, the jagged point pressing on the nerve in my jaw makes me writhe with pain. But the pain reminds me I'm alive.

I find a space on the wall. The ground may look dead as ancient skin, but dig down, further than you ever thought you could with the half-broken tools they give you, and suddenly you come upon riches: a cluster of spiky treasure, nestling in its soft, earthy hole like spider's eggs. When you find it don't shout; don't speak; don't even breathe. Let the raucousness of the mine surround you; cloak you. Feel the slowly quickening pulse in your fingertips, almost numb from days, months, years of probing the skin of the soil as thoroughly as a woman searching for scars on her lover. Chip the gems out, by hand or tool. Rub them clean; hold them; watch the surfaces catch the light. Then get ready to hand them over.

Apparently this place is unusual: the deposits are plentiful and easy to reach, but the stones are small. Still, useful enough to the government for income; and punishment. At least we're not underground; although in the heat of the day I sometimes long for the cool dark of a tunnel. But then I imagine the bodies, packed in together, and how quickly the air would become stifling. Out here I can breathe, even if it's dust and diesel fumes.

You have to focus your whole being on the wall, searching for a seam, a way in. But look outwards too. If someone stops suddenly, facing the earth, he has found a stone, and is weighing up his chances of hiding it. If a man backs away from the wall, slowly, as if dazed, he has started to see red dust behind his eyes; when he turns and looks round, shapes will be darkened blurs. His pitch will soon be for the taking.

At this hour the air is still cold. To pass the time I sing: a monotonous chant, some long-lost injustice from our forgotten past. Who are we all, anyway? Nothing but a collection of desperate people, who have ended up here by chance – bad chance – and are unlikely ever to leave.

Haven't you guessed why? I'll give you an idea: Tiko, whose red bandana hides the scar at his neck, had been asked to look after his neighbour's three children. He raped and murdered them, and then set fire to the house to cover his tracks. Raneek, over there – he turned his blank gaze on me, just then – killed his brother-in-law for a bet. Vevan, who is lying in the dirt, moaning – he worked in a home for old people and slowly starved them to death. There are many more stories. My own? Maybe later.

I spread my palms flat on the wall, working out where to dig. I've seen others copying me, but get it wrong. If they hit a fault line, in the blink of a blistered eye the red wall breaks away and shifts downwards, sending up choking clouds. It's impressive, even to those of us who have seen it before: the moment the earth reminds us of its power. Where men once perched, the cliff recreates itself, revealing new outcrops and ridges; new possibilities. The survivors stand around or balance on ledges, covering their mouths and eyes against the dust. Before it settles they are back, swarming through the moving air and clawing at the soil; searching, not for still-warm bodies, but any seam that may have been revealed by the fall.

That's the logic of the mine.

Sure enough, out of the corner of my eye I see Mino, a young, eager worker – he still thinks he'll get out alive! – watching me. When I stare at him, instead of turning away he gives me an odd smile. I keep my eye on him all morning but I see nothing unusual. Then suddenly he jerks, and bends double. Liquid runs on the ground, and I smell the familiar stench. The food doesn't agree with him. He'll get used to it. I was the same when I started.

* * *

At midday there is a grinding, roaring noise from the lip of the mine. Despite myself I look up. The food is coming down. Black clouds of flies hang round the metal buckets. The ripe, slightly sour smell of the meat fills the air.

I move quickly out of the shade, along a narrow path at the foot of the cliff. The heat is a blunt weapon on my skin. In front of the platform where the buckets sit in the sun, men are being pushed back by the guards.

"Lucas!" One of them waves his whip. "Mackenzie says you go first today."

"Bastard!" a nearby voice mutters. A gob of spit lands by my bare foot. I tense, waiting for the fight, but nothing happens. I'm shoved to the front. Vevan and Raneek exchange a look but say nothing. I untie my tin plate from my belt and the man doles out a ladle of beans, dotted with grey meat. The first thing I'll do when I get out is eat steak.

But the meal gives me strength. I return to the wall. Under my hands the cliff face seems to move. My fingers caress the crumbling earth. Somewhere long ago, in another world, white linen billows at an open window – on the breeze, the scent of frangipani and sweet orange blossom. Down the narrow cobbled street lie the blue waters of a bay. And in the bed, the white linen bed, the cool breeze playing over it, are brown limbs. Slender, smooth: perfect as a baby's. I press my hand against the red earth and see only her startled face; her eyes, the whites wide at first, green pupils huge as newly polished emeralds. The unlined forehead, the dark hair. The look of terror. The noises – gasping, grunting. Something went wrong. And then it was too late. But I've paid the price. Now, under my fingers is an unmistakeable, hard edge. I can't suppress a shudder of excitement. A quick look around assures me that no one is watching. Not even Mino. He is fighting over what's left of the food.

I push my hands deeper into the earth. I grasp, and feel, then check, looking round carefully; then I lean in close, pressing my mouth to the wall, so that when I breathe, fine dust catches in my throat. I kiss the soil like a long-forgotten lover. What was her name? It has gone with her, into oblivion.

The unforgiving stone is in my mouth. Then it's easy – I have practised long and hard. It slides into the hole in my tooth, and sticks. The familiar stab signals treasure; secret.

A rumour is spreading like sickness through the mine. Something has changed, at the top. A new device, a machine, has been installed. Whatever the contraption, it can detect hidden gems.

"Someone is stealing again," says Geron, who has come to work next to me. His good eye scours the surface for the glint of a seam. He turns towards me, his left eye socket hollow under its flap of skin. "I hear they know who it is."

"Is it Mino?" I ask. He would be good to get rid of.

"The new machine will find it," he says, his hands fluttering, showering earth like dried blood.

I feel the edge of the stolen stone with my tongue. I can taste blood. I turn away and spit on my palm. My heart jumps about under my ribs. I push at the gem with my tongue. It is stuck, tightly wedged.

"What is this new machine?" I hate having to use Geron as my informant, but it would attract too much attention to ask someone else. I wipe my mouth with my hand.

He shrugs. "It can find any gem, any size," he says. "Hidden anywhere, even inside a body."

But we both know no one would try that again. The memory of Lieno's death is too recent.

"Lieno was unlucky," I whisper. I swallow hard.

Geron turns his one-eyed gaze on me.

My tongue probes my tooth. I shove my fingers into my mouth: a suspicious gesture. I cannot pull the stone out.

I claw at the cliff face: if I caused a landfall, that might be enough diversion to occupy the overseers for the rest of the day. But nothing moves.

By the end of the day, I have found another small stone. I grasp it in my palm. I'll hold this new stone as I approach the machine, whatever it is. If the machine finds the hidden gem, I'll show Mackenzie the one in my palm: say I was testing it for him; as usual, I've done him a favour.

The siren screams. In the fading light we fight for position at the bottom of the cliff, bruised and cut skin against skin. The rope ladder creeps down the rock face, through the dusk, like a snake descending into its coil; the opposite of a rope trick I saw, years ago, in a square under a hot, dry sun.

Through gaps in the cloud today the sky was turquoise, aquamarine; the colour of that bay, where the ship sailed without me, long ago. In the morning I'll leave. To see the ocean once more: to try again.

The ladder swings down. I am at the front, Mino and Geron behind me. Before they can move I grab the rope. Suddenly, everyone falls back and I'm swaying, up, up, under the cloud, alone. Why don't they follow me? I look down. Dirt-streaked faces are turned towards me. But they're not angry. They're smiling. It's too high now to jump off; the ladder is being winched up faster, with only me clinging to it. The gem I have found is safe in my pocket. The other is wedged in my mouth.

I reach the mine lip. The overseers have been busy – behind an arch made of metal struts, a tunnel of hammered sheet iron leads into the dusk. The machine must be at the end of it. The machine I saw on the truck.

"Lucas!" Mackenzie is awake, upright; his rifle at his shoulder. His face is unreadable. "Walk through." His gaze slides away from me.

"Hey, comrade! This is me, right?"

"Walk through," he repeats. He pushes me.

"Why?" I put my hand in my pocket. Should I take the stone out now? How does the machine work? If I show it too soon... I run my tongue over my teeth.

"New rules," Mackenzie mutters. "Walk through." He lifts his rifle.

"How does it work?" I want to ask him, but my mouth is full of blood. I have to move. I drag my feet over the flattened earth and into the tunnel. It's dark. Fear prickles the back of my neck. From nowhere comes the memory of Lieno: his gasp when the knife went in. That wasn't what I intended. I thought Mackenzie would wait; let nature do the job. I see again the skinny, writhing body, suddenly still in the dust.

I keep walking. My eyes adjust and I notice a winking light. Nothing happens. In my mouth, I feel the stone suddenly come loose. I cough, trying to hawk it up, but it's too late. It slides down my throat.

As I gasp for air, an alarm sounds.

The Trees

Melanie Susan Marshall

The trees high up on Brunel's Trail occupy Jacob's thoughts. A dozen ash trees standing in a line, visible from every window with their medusa heads and grizzled bark. Just vegetation, he tells himself again and again. Just hard wood, part of nature, not twisted or malformed.

He'd met Ellie at the folk house in the spring. There, under her tuition, he perfected bluegrass guitar. After each lesson he'd let his coffee go cold just to sit with her (she favoured a pot of rooibos and the Welsh apple cake). It was the only place they were safe to joke, inside those walls festooned with woodblock prints. By September he was untangling her limbs against those trees, then plucking her hairs from his shirt, masking the constant smell of sex with Lynx. "Ash trees heal," she'd say in his ear, before dragging her nails over his shoulder. "Pass through a split tree and you'll become a new man." He couldn't believe he'd fallen for someone who believed in shit like that, but frankly he didn't care back then.

Lies fell from him and scattered on the ground, tripping him up when Lucy asked him questions. Lucy, the one he still hadn't proposed to, worked at the Royal Infirmary. On the rare occasions he did see her awake these days, her eyes were clouded by NHS horizons and she spoke in monotone. When he returned home after that first time with Ellie, even her standard issue uniforms faded from blue to grey on the clotheshorse. How long had she been like this? Hardly a shadow of that girl dressed as a devil who'd flogged him vodka shots for a quid each at Freshers' fair. He wished it could be different, knew that it was just as much his fault: staying up late, smoking too much, leaving washing moldering in the machine.

He wakes alone as the little hand clicks to eleven, his mouth laced with Lidl whisky and lager. Toothpaste tastes wrong, tea wronger. He stares out the window a while, wondering if he'll write a song today. Possibly not. Their flat is at the top of the hill near the downs and theirs is clearest of views (not that Lucy bothers to look). Far in the distance is the line of trees. Spindly now, middle aged and losing their foliage, but these are the branches and twigs that claw at the windowpane of his dreams. The outline of them cuts deep into the sky. In the day they're the darkest black and by night the moon makes them glow. There's no hiding from them. Sometimes he'll be practicing chords, or buying milk or cracking one off to the sound of his randy neighbours going at it and suddenly there the trees are in his head, a procession of magistrates and a rush of sawdust scent — and he's a cheat, a bastard, a disappointment. It's tricky to carry on when that happens. At work he often feigned a migraine, which is probably why he was asked to leave in the end.

Well, he'll put a stop to it, today. He reaches for his battered mobile, texts Ellie. *Meet at the bridge?* Of course she will. He puts on his trainers, and a scarf over his denim jacket to stave off the chill, then he's off to end this thing once and for all — whatever it has become. Down the alley, past the chip shop and into a street of gift shops and hardware stores, brushing by cauliflowers on the veg stall, he takes a shortcut through the unwelcome new Tesco and strides down the vertiginous hill to the centre.

Ellie's already there waiting for him. Of course she is. She recently cropped her hair, perhaps at the complaint that he kept finding long strands everywhere. It makes her eyes icier, her chin cuter somehow. She's drumming her fingers on the railings, guitar bag burdening her shoulders – focused on the swans and fag butts floating along the river. Sunlight glints from the vintage marcasite watch he bought her in Old Market. Not a bribe, not a sweetener he told himself as he handed over the remainder his overdraft. In the centre he can't see the trees, nobody can. But they can see him, with surveillance greater than the city's CCTV.

"'Lo," Ellie says. "How you feeling this morning?"

Drawing back from the first kiss of the new day he notices a spot between her eyebrows. Not that a pimple will make it any easier to also call this their final kiss.

"Alright. Can we go somewhere quiet?" Aware of shoppers and toddlers and newspaper sellers, people he doesn't know and those he might.

"Pub or mine?" She asks, as though this is a proper choice.

"Could go for one in the Duke, if you have money?"

She nods, wraps her cardi a little tighter. "Brrr. Won't be long 'til winter."

He sets off by her side, looking over his shoulder.

"What time did you get in last night then?" she asks.

He pretends to ponder. "Dunno. Gone four. It was light anyway." He shakes off the image of branches multiplying against the dawn sky and thinks instead of the remnants of kebab he left on the wall.

The sun goes in as they walk, not hand-in-hand, past the church obliterated by bombs in the war, through the park that once served as its graveyard. The flowers are dead. The leaves crackle underfoot.

She looks up at him. Her cheeks are pinked with either blusher or cold, he can't tell which. "Moles Club gig on Friday night. I'm getting nervous, Alex says it's gonna be a big crowd."

The gig. He said he'd be there. He promised. "It'll be fine," he says.

She shrugs. He lights a pre-rolled fag and Ellie shares it with him. All Lucy shares with him is an abundance of cancerous literature on the dangers of tobacco. Jacob's fingers twitch as he passes the rollie to her. Even watching her funny lipless mouth folding around the cigarette – that mouth which usually does so much for him – is no distraction.

The Duke of York is inhabited by Crazy Joe on his stool and a group of students in skinny jeans shooting pool. Ellie umms and ahhs then orders cheesy chips with her pint. She likes to eat. Lucy follows the Department of Health's recommended guidelines to a T, the units of alcohol, the grams of salt.

He watches Ellie exchanging pleasantries with the barman. How easy it is to be here with her. How separate from his life with Lucy. Of course, the Catholic expectations of his mum and dad weighed on him from the start. To them, co-habiting is marginally more acceptable than buggery and they only appreciate Lucy on the basis that she is for certain the mother of their future grandchildren. Fair, freckled munchkins with empty heads into which they can stuff their doctrine. And Lucy isn't some struggling musician who only showers every other day for eco reasons. They'd probably say they did not spend seventeen grand a year on his schooling for him to spend his days shit-faced and getting his end away. And never mind his and Lucy's mutual friends – Phil and Susannah, Jen and Sean, Alex and Becca. The ones who cook confit de canard and pour Chateauneuf Du Pape because it was sooo incredibly ironic to 'play' grown ups, he could hear them now: *But you were so perfect together… but you were going to be our best man…you were going to be godparents to William… why would you do that, you fucking loser…*

He pauses the imaginary outrage. Reality spoke for itself: on Thursday Lucy arrived home less than ten minutes after Ellie had hoiked up her knickers, buttoned her shirt and left. He can't take that risk again.

He picks a seat in the furthest corner from the bar, near the toilets. A modicum of light seeps through the window. And there, past the stained net curtains, that remind him of his girlfriend's 'lingerie'… He blinks. It can't be possible, geographically. Can it? Brunel's Trail is visible from this window. He shivers. They should really light the fire in here. The table is cold and lifeless wood beneath his hands. Carved with names, insults, cocks big and small.

Ellie sets down her guitar against the wall and his Guinness on the table. The black stuff is the only booze he can stomach the day after, something to do with the Irish in his blood. It's wrong that she's just bought him a drink and now he's going to… He inhales the piss and beer and B.O. and begins.

"Ellie." Saying it is weird enough, they rarely refer to each other by name. She looks up, all bluebell eyes.

"Don't tell me. You want us to go for a little 'walk' later," she says, eyebrow arched. "Drink up then. If you go *up* to the woods today…"

"No, listen…"

Her chips arrive. She picks one up, blows away the steam and slides it between her lips.

"I…I've been thinking," Jacob continues. Sprigs scrape at the maze of his brain. "The band's starting to take off and you're going to need to spend more time concentrating on the music." Bad, bad angle, what is he doing? She stares back. "Listen, the thing is, I think Lucy suspects."

Ellie flinches a tiny bit.

"She just knows, you know. She's not thick. And I'm not around an awful lot. I think it would be better if…"

Ellie lets a mushed-up mouthful of chip fall back into the bowl. "Hot" she says. He's about to deliver the closing sentence when a shadow falls across the table. A pillar of green and brown. Panic rises in his gullet.

"Jake?" No one calls him that. "It is you! I thought it was you!" The hulk of green wool is Ann from the office; he hasn't seen her since he was fired.

He nods. If he doesn't speak maybe she'll go away.

"How wonderful to see you. What have you been up to since… that awful business?…And this must be the lovely Lucy."

The last gulp of stout lubricates his throat enough to croak, "Not Lucy, just a friend."

Ellie scowls.

"Well I won't keep you; how goes the music, it's that country and western you play isn't it?"

"Bluegrass," he says. "Good thanks." Ann nods, then turns and waves on her way back to the bar.

"Sorry," Jacob says. "I'll get us something to take the edge off." Then as he's walking away he remembers, "Got any money left?" Ellie shakes her head. He feels Lucy's Visa in his pocket and recollects the pin, her mother's year of birth. For all Lucy knows he could be sharing a drink with Phil or Sean or Alex. He returns with two tumblers of whisky. Ellie downs hers.

"You're choosing good little nursey over what you really want, again. It's not good for the soul."

"I don't know what I want."

" 'S about time you make up your bloody mind." She gets up, runs a hand through the remainder of her hair as if feeling for the ghost of it. "Home time. You coming?" She leaves half-eaten chips and empty glasses on the table.

To his left, Jacob can feel them. Tree limbs, gaunt hands. Distorted through the curtain. The distance between the hill and the pub has shortened, he's sure of it. He screws up his eyes, but the trees are still there. When he opens his eyes, Crazy Joe is gawping at him. He hurries after Ellie.

As soon as she's in her t-shirt and pants he wants to feast on her. Harvest some of that passion to use in later years. Hibernate in the month-old sheets. Ellie's bedsit gives off a fug of old books and something vinegary. The place is probably a health hazard, but sometimes just thinking about the smell makes him hard.

"After," she whispers. "After, we can talk."

Jacob shuts the door, in case her mongrel Bandit is loose in the building again. On her bed, beneath the window, Ellie is lying on her back. Jacob peels black cotton away from her skin. Reveals the feather tattooed across her hipbone. In this light it could be a leaf. It undulates as she moves up the bed towards the pillow. Curls and crinkles at the edges. She laughs. The ritual is familiar – more so even than with Lucy because with Ellie he likes to remember it, likes to think about what he does, what she's doing – the biting of her bottom lip, the clasping at his balls. But this will be the last time. Sweat gathers; breath solidifies. The darkness of the room isn't as dark as it was. The slice between the curtains has widened. He closes his eyes and concentrates on the actions, not on the feeling, not the feeling… as he gains momentum, her thighs urge against him, fleshy thighs for such a small body, she reaches up behind her, her hands entwine with the pine bedposts.

He clutches her hips, the side of her waist oddly rough to the touch, the fissures and ridges of stretch marks around her where she grew so fast as a teenager. They kiss open-mouthed and sloppy, but he can't look at her right now in case it tips him over the edge, so he looks up instead, holding on. The curtains are wide apart. He is so sure they were drawn shut when they started. Over the bed, through the glass, grey shapes. One by one they appear in the haze, moving from fuzzy to definite around the edges, twelve trees…he's not a rational man, he's not thinking straight…he's…. His mind splits in two as he comes. She's far behind and he can't carry on, rolling off and over in crumpled sheets. He hopes there's something like apology in his kiss.

'Don't worry,' she murmurs and closes her eyes. She's got what she wanted, he thinks, because I haven't left her yet. He touches her Eagles t-shirt balled up by the pillow and then strokes up her breasts and shoulders and over her cropped hair. A sharp thing stabs his hand. Between thumb and forefinger he extracts the offending article – a tiny splinter of twig.

At six thirty, he leaves a stumbles out onto the street. He has to see Lucy. He stops off at the shop and picks up a pizza for dinner, and then returns to the chilled aisle for some salad to go with it, leaving the coins spinning at the checkout. Wades through the cans and Cadbury's wrappers that carpet the pavements. Geese flap in V formation overhead. He waits beneath the sign that says Royal Infirmary and several doctors and office workers march past. An ambulance lurches around the corner coating the concrete in blue light. At gone ten to, Lucy finally emerges. Her expression is serious as though she is evaluating her day's work, but pretty all the same.

She smiles when she spots him. "Aww darling, you met me from work?"

"Yes," he says. "And I got dinner."

She glances at the Tesco bag. "But I'm having dinner with Jen tonight, remember?"

"Oh." He's shaking and not sure if from cold or something else.

"Are you OK?"

Yes, he's fine. What to say? He doesn't love her? He's leaving her? He's staying with her for all eternity? She plants a kiss on his lips. "Urgh, you smell funny," she says, laughing.

He backs away. "How was your shift?"

"All suicide attempts and flu patients. A few bruised women to patch up and send back to abusive partners." Her expression drops. "How was your day? Get anything from the temping agency?"

He shakes his head.

"Oh well, you'll find something soon."

He looks at her, really looks. And wonders why he's even there. "Are you going home first?" he asks.

"Yeah, to have a shower and change."

"Could you take this then," he hands her the shopping bags.

"Where're you off to?" she asks.

"Just fancy a bit of fresh air."

Lucy smiles, steps closer. He holds his breath, trying to anticipate what she'll do or say. She reaches over and brushes a strand of his hair from his eyes. "Sure. See you later."

He hollows out inside as she walks away, her shoulders straight, her ponytail swinging. The ache is an alien one to him - to be a different person completely. His twelve accusers scorch the inside of his eyelids. He needs to think. He needs *somewhere* to think. If they want him that badly then he'll go to them. Ellie's mystical crap rings in his ears... a new man, that's what he wants to be more than anything. A new man.

Jacob knows the direction although he's never walked there, only been driven in Ellie's Fiesta. He has no money for a bus, not that the city buses go that far. Up the Bath Road, past the library, through St George and out through the sprawl, climbing up and up to the brim of the hill. Hunger nips at his stomach, but it's not important. The evening brings rain. Water courses down his face and neck and soaks through the denim of his jacket. He trudges on. The trees flicker and shake on the skyline, backlit by light pollution. Headlights slide past. A 4x4 plunges into a puddle by the verge and it's too late to jump out the way. The wave drenches him and he gasps for breath spluttering bilge and bits of leaves. Through the torrent in front of his eyes Brunel's Trail looms. Perhaps he could turn back. He looks behind him and can't see the path, it is so obscured by bramble and furze and downpour.

He clutches the piece of twig in his pocket. The first time they'd driven up there they kidded themselves they were just taking Bandit for a walk. Simply talking and strolling in the late sunshine; the Durex in his wallet just a talisman. Ellie ran her hands all over the bark like some sort of crazed wood nymph. She kissed him. That was right, she kissed him first – standing on tiptoe and ignoring his "I've got a girlfriend" line, before scampering off and skulking behind branches, flinging off her hoodie and top and shouting, "And I taught you guitar, you owe me," the words echoing from each tree. He tied the dog's lead to a gatepost and followed her along the line of trees. "The spacing between each one is perfect. They must have been hand-planted, it can't happen like that naturally," she said. "Sssh, c'm here," was all he had said, as he unbuttoned the flies of his jeans.

They fucked on the ground, stones in his knees and soil on his hands. But that wasn't good for her. She extricated her pale body from his and pressed her back up against the farthest trunk from the road; number twelve.

The night thickens. He traipses through the forest floor, heavy with leaves. His sodden socks stick to his feet. From what he can see by the torch on his mobile, his feet, ankles and legs are slathered in mud. Everything is a shade of black: he can only tell dark from light. Beaten by rain and heavier now, he trudges on. Across the field, battered stalks cast shadows. Right near, a rustling and flapping in the undergrowth. His heart drums. A pigeon lands on a bough, its feathers slick.

He can see the trunk outlines so clear up above now. The final stretch awaits, a vertical climb. Dodging boulders and sidestepping clumps of nettles, he scales the hill. Brambles leap out and thorns attack his bare hands. He's mad, he should get a job; he's kidding himself. Stupid trees. He clambers up and up. His foot hits something hard, a rock or root perhaps. His Converse soles slip once, twice under him. He can't find his footing on the scree beneath... He flails, grasping for whatever's near, grabs at dead cow parsley that breaks off in his hands like wet cardboard, and he's tumbling down. The twelve trees revolve on their axis as he falls.

He lands on his side. He props himself up. The side of his face is stinging and studded with grit. Water streams in his eyes. The back of his head feels dull. He reaches to touch his hair. His sore fingers are wet and black and taste of iron. He moves to get up and pain spears his ankle. Staying seated awkwardly like that with one leg under him, the other outstretched, he forces his lungs to take air in and out. It hurts. He should give up the fags.

The trees mock from the peak of the hill. He drags himself back up the slope, crawling through mud, arms and legs stiff, ankle throbbing. Queasiness rises in his gut. He's never been one to deal with pain well. He heaves himself up the bank to where they grow. The nearest trunk is close enough to touch. He sits between the two middle trees in an unwieldy position trying not to move his leg, trying to get his breath back. Clumps of rain flop on his hair. The city burns below like an upside-down sky.

He'll propose to Lucy with a fifty quid ring. Will that satisfy everyone? No, he'll take Ellie travelling in South America – far from anyone he knows. Plus they have different trees there, he's sure. With what money he'll do these things he doesn't know. Pulling up his trouser leg he shines the phone down at his ankle. Ruptured skin and a lump protruding where it shouldn't. Shock thumps the back of his neck and he gags and retches into the earth. Spit dangles from his lips. Better that he just gets rid and moves up North, just him and his guitar. That's what he'll do. Leave them both to it. Tomorrow, when Lucy's at work. But Ellie's fingers strumming the strings. Ellie's legs in the sun. Ellie naked against the bark.

He shines the light on the bark of the tree next to him. How would you pass through the split of a tree, anyway? He smoothes it with his hand. Contours, shapes of graffitied letters, lichen and slime, notches like eyes, peeling, grey as old bone. Along the row, left and right, the others stand. He returns the phone to his pocket. He'd rather not see them. He sits, arms and legs outstretched on the leaf-suffocated ground. His foot sinks though the foliage and into the soft mire with a squelch. He finds that it cools and deadens his ankle. He buries each hand, each foot deeper, like into the sandpit as a kid. Suction pulls and tows beneath the mud.

The rain has eased to a patter. He can hear his own breathing. If he just concentrates on that, the pain abates. He should go back, get help. Maybe he'll have a quick fag, if his baccy's not drenched. Maybe he'll call Ellie first. Or an ambulance. He goes to retrieve his right hand from the pit of earth in which it's buried. It's stuck. His brain tells it to move. It remains. He tries to shift his unhurt foot from its hole. *Move.* It doesn't. The wrench of the earth keeps him in place. He feels its mass dragging him down. His hands, his feet lodged between the roots. His four limbs solidify. Numb. His weight spreads into the hill. *I can't move, I can't move, Ican'tmove.* The wind picks up again.

One Way Ticket to Mexico

Annie Mfula

Céline slowly slipped her dress back on. She knew that Mark was watching her. She pinned up her dark hair then went to the dressing mirror to touch up her crimson lipstick. She smiled when she saw Mark's reflection in the mirror.

"Are you sure you don't want me to get back into bed Mr. Symanski?" she asked him.

"That's very tempting darling, but best not. We don't have much time left," said Mark. He got out of bed and started to get dressed. Céline walked up to him and gave him a lingering kiss.

"We still have an hour or so," she said. Mark gently pushed Céline away.

"Yes, and we're going to use that hour to go over the plan one last time," said Mark. Céline turned away from Mark and crossed her arms like a petulant child.

"I'm sick of talking about the plan!" she said. "Are you ready to do ten years in prison? Because that's what we're facing if anything goes wrong," said Mark. Céline didn't respond. She lit a cigarette and took a deep drag. "Look darling, I just want to make sure that everything goes to plan, so that we can be together. Isn't that what you want?" asked Mark.

"Yes, off course," said Céline.

"Good! So let's go over it again. Oh, and put that cigarette out will you? You know I hate it when you smoke," said Mark. Céline sighed and pushed her cigarette into an ashtray.

"Right, let's start from the beginning. Talk me through it," said Mark. Céline sat down at the end of the bed whilst Mark paced up and down the hotel room.

"I'm working the afternoon shift tomorrow, so I'll leave my flat at 10.30am. I need to make sure that I follow my usual routine," said Céline.

"And what's your usual routine?" asked Mark.

"Get the tube into town, buy lunch at the French Salad Bar, and then eat in the staff room with the others," said Céline.

"Good! So, you'll start your shift at 12pm. You and Susannah will work the windows and Maggie will work the customer floor. Make sure you don't do anything unusual, nothing to draw attention to yourself," said Mark.

"Alright," said Céline.

"Good! What next?" Mark asked.

"By the time it's 4.55pm the bank will be empty. You'll come round and ask whose turn it is to lock the doors. I'll say it's my turn," said Céline.

"Right, then I'll take Susannah and Maggie to my office to help me balance the cash. What next?" Mark asked.

"As I go to lock the door, Suleiman will storm into the bank. He'll be wearing a balaclava and he'll have a gun. He'll drag me into the back and he'll ask me to identify the bank manager. I'll point at you," said Céline.

"Good, and then what?" asked Mark.

"Suleiman will hand me some rope and ask me to tie up Maggie and Susannah. Then he'll ask me to lie down on the floor and he'll tie me up," said Céline.

"Yes, and make sure the knots are tight when you tie up Maggie and Susannah. The last thing we want is them running off and sounding the silent alarm," said Mark.

"I will," said Céline.

"After Suleiman has tied you up, he'll force me to open the vault and I'll give him all the money. Then, he'll take me hostage. We'll leave together through the back exit. We'll take my car," said Mark.

Céline rubbed her temple in slow circular motions.

"What's wrong?" asked Mark. He sat down and put his arm around her.

"I'm just worried Mark. What if something goes wrong?" asked Céline.

"Nothing will go wrong. I told you, Suleiman's a fool. When we leave the bank, we'll drive to the industrial park on Japp Street. We'll ditch my car and take his. I'll give him some money and drop him off near the train station like we agreed. After that, I'll drive to his hovel of a flat and plant the evidence. Then, I'll drive back towards the train station, ditch his car and stagger into the street all bruised and traumatised. When the police turn up, I'll tell them about Suleiman and the robbery. The CCTV footage will back up our story. The police will focus all their attention on Suleiman. By the time they figure out what really happened, you and I will be in Mexico," said Mark. He kissed Céline's hand. "When you get home tonight, pack a bag. As soon as the police have finished interviewing you tomorrow, go home and wait for me. I'll come and get you. We'll take the Eurostar to Paris. You can say bye to your family and then we'll catch a flight to Mexico City," said Mark.

Mark looked down at his watch. "Darling look, I have to go," he said.

"Back home to your wife?" snapped Céline. Mark tried not to rise to Céline's gibe.

"Don't start that again Céline," he said. He stood up and put his coat on.

"Well how do you expect me to feel? Knowing that you're going home to her!" said Céline.

"But, you know that I don't love Julie," said Mark.

"Then why are you still married to her?" asked Céline.

"For heaven's sake Céline, we've been through this. I couldn't divorce her. She's a lawyer for Pete's sake! She'd have taken me to the cleaners," said Mark. His face softened when he saw the wounded look on Céline's face.

"Darling, I don't know why we're even arguing about this. It doesn't matter any more. By tomorrow evening, it'll be just you and me," he said.

"I'm just tired of hiding our relationship from everybody Mark," said Céline.

"Me too darling, but it won't be for much longer I promise. Now, I really have to go," said Mark.

"Alright, I'll just get my coat," said Céline.

"No, we can't be seen leaving together. You stay here for ten minutes and then leave. I'll call you later," said Mark. He gave Céline a kiss and left.

Ten minutes later, Céline put her dark glasses on and walked out of the hotel. She kept her head down as she made her way to the nearest tube station. The reality of what she was about to do started to sink in. Suddenly, Céline felt as though everyone was watching her. By the time she walked through the front door of her flat, she was shaking. She lit a cigarette and reached for the mobile phone that Mark had given her. She started to dial his number, but then changed her mind and threw the phone back down. Get a grip Céline, she thought. She ran herself a hot bath and tried to relax. Soon, she would have everything that she wanted. She would have money and she would have Mark. She felt a twinge of guilt over double crossing Suleiman, but she brushed it aside. He was a career criminal. He'd been inside for burglary, serious assault, car theft. A man like that needed to be in prison.

By the time Mark phoned, Céline was on her second packet of cigarettes. "You sound strange," he said.

"I'm scared Mark," said Céline. "There's nothing to worry about. Everything's ready," said Mark.

"Suleiman?" asked Céline.

"He'll walk into the bank at 4.58pm as planned," said Mark.

"I've got a really bad feeling something will go wrong," said Céline.

"Nothing will go wrong. Just do your part and I'll do mine, alright," said Mark.

"Alright," said Céline.

"Darling, I have to go. Try and get some rest," said Mark.

"I will. I love you," said Céline.

"Me too," said Mark.

It was another 6 hours before Céline finally drifted off into a restless sleep. When her alarm went off at 8am, she felt worn out. After a long shower and some very strong coffee, Céline left her flat. This is my last commute, she thought as she got the tube into town. She stopped at the French Salad Bar and bought a walnut and blue cheese salad. Maggie and Susannah were already in the staff room having lunch when Céline walked into the bank. She struggled to eat hers.

"Are you alright Céline? You've hardly touched your food," said Maggie.

"I had an upset stomach this morning. It's affected my appetite," said Céline.

"Make sure you take plenty of fluids, love. That always helps," said Susannah. Céline's heart jumped when Mark walked into the staff room.

"Morning ladies," he said.

"Good morning Mr. Symanski," Maggie and Susannah replied in unison.

"Let's hurry things up in here. It's almost time for shift changeover," said Mark. He poured himself a cup of coffee, then left.

"His wife is one very lucky lady," said Susannah. Not for much longer, thought Céline.

Céline kept a keen eye on the clock as she worked through her shift. Her anxiety grew with each hour that passed. At 4.55pm, Mark walked casually onto the empty customer floor.

"It's closing time, ladies. Whose turn is it to lock up?" he asked. Céline responded quickly.

"I think it's my turn," she said.

"Fine, Céline you lock up. Maggie and Susannah, you're on cash duty with me," said Mark. Mark took Susannah and Maggie to his office, leaving Céline on her own. Her world descended into slow motion as she walked towards the door. She faltered when she saw Suleiman. He was dressed in black, his face hidden behind a balaclava. He pushed the door open and pointed a gun at Céline.

"Don't scream," he said quietly. Céline started to tremble. "Lock the door," said Suleiman. Céline did as he asked. Suleiman grabbed Céline's arm. "Now, get in the back," he said. Maggie and Susannah screamed when they saw Suleiman and the gun. Mark got slowly to his feet.

"Alright mate, whoever you are, just take it easy," he said to Suleiman.

"Don't tell me to take it easy. Get down on the floor now!" shouted Suleiman. Maggie and Susannah scrambled onto the floor. Mark did the same. "Which one's the bank manager?" Suleiman asked Céline. Céline gestured towards Mark. Suleiman handed her some rope.

"Tie those two women up," he said. Céline bound Maggie and Susannah's hands and feet as tightly as she could. "Now get down onto the floor with the others," Suleiman said to her. He bound her hands and feet loosely. "Don't move or try anything stupid," said Suleiman. His menacing tone sent a chill through Céline. Suleiman stashed the money in Mark's office into a bag then he dragged Mark to his feet. "You're going to take me to the vault and after that we'll go for a nice little drive," he said. Suleiman marched Mark out of the office.

"We're going to die," sobbed Susannah.

"We're not going to die. We'll be fine," whispered Céline.

"Poor Mark. Do you think he's alright?" whispered Maggie. Céline fought back her guilt.

"I'm sure Mark will be fine too," she whispered.

Céline broke into a cold sweat when the police turned up just forty minutes later. It was much too soon. Don't panic Céline, she thought. Even if Mark hadn't managed to plant some evidence at Suleiman's flat, she was still in the clear. And, so was Mark. They were just the traumatised victims of the robbery. The lead detective was a man called Hughes. He took separate statements from Maggie, then Susannah and lastly Céline. Céline's voice quivered as she gave him her version of events.

"Thank you Miss Molyneux, I think I have everything I need for now," said Detective Hughes.

"Does that mean I can go home?" asked Céline.

"Not just yet," said Detective Hughes. A uniformed policeman pulled Detective Hughes to one side. Céline felt the hairs on the back of her neck stand on end as she watched them. They spoke in hushed tones and then turned and looked at her. Detective Hughes approached Céline.

"I'd like to ask you some more questions Miss Molyneux, down at the station," he said. Céline's throat went dry.

"What questions?" she whispered.

"Just come with me please Miss Molyneux," said Detective Hughes. Céline couldn't bring herself to look at Maggie and Susannah as she was led to the police car.

Céline had to endure an hour long wait alone in an interview room when they reached the police station. Just stick to your story, she told herself. Detective Hughes and his colleague Detective Freeman eventually came in to question her. Céline jumped when Detective Hughes slammed a file onto the table.

"Sorry to keep you waiting Miss Molyneux," he said.

"What's this about?" asked Céline.

"I'd strongly advise you to have a lawyer present during this interview Miss Molyneaux. I can arrange it for you," said Detective Hughes. Céline raised her head in defiance.

"I don't need a lawyer. I have nothing to hide," she said. Detective Hughes switched on the recorder.

"Interview commenced at 8pm. Present, Detective Hughes, Detective Freeman and Miss Céline Molyneux," he stated. Detective Hughes sat back in his seat. "Miss Molyneux, would you like to retract the statement you made earlier and tell me the truth?" he asked.

"I already told you the truth," said Céline.

"So you're sticking to your statement?" asked Detective Freeman.

"Yes," said Céline. Detectives Hughes and Freeman

exchanged a glance.

"You'll be glad to hear Miss Molyneux that we've found Mr. Symanski," said Detective Freeman.

"Is he alright?" asked Céline.

"Yes, apart from a few cuts and bruises. It was nice of you and your accomplice to show Mr. Symanski some compassion," said Detective Hughes. Beads of sweat formed on Céline's brow.

"I don't know what you're talking about," she said.

"Sure you do Miss Molyneux. After all, you planned this whole thing. You and your friend in the balaclava," said Detective Freeman.

"No, I have nothing to do with this," said Céline.

"Miss Molyneux, your balaclava'd friend himself identified you as his accomplice," said Detective Freeman.

"You've arrested him?" asked Céline.

"Not yet, but it's only a matter of time," said Detective Freeman.

"Then how can he have identified me?" asked Céline.

"He let slip whilst he was holding Mr. Symanski hostage," said Detective Hughes. Céline shook her head.

"No, he's lying! Whatever he said, he's lying!" she said.

"Who's lying, Miss Molyneux?" asked Detective Hughes.

"Suleiman! I mean, the man in the balaclava," stuttered Céline.

"So you have nothing to do with this, and yet you know his name?" asked Detective Molyneux. Céline didn't respond. Her head was spinning.

"Miss Molyneux, if I were you I'd start talking. The evidence against you is overwhelming," said Detective Hughes.

"What evidence?" asked Céline.

"The evidence in your flat Miss Molyneux. We've just come from there. We found the bank floor plans, the mobile phone you used to communicate with your accomplice and your suitcase, packed and ready to skip the country," said Detective Hughes. Céline's face paled. Suddenly, everything was clear.

"They've set me up," she whispered.

"Who's set you up Miss Molyneux?" asked Detective Freeman. "Mark and Suleiman," said Céline.

"Mark? You mean Mr. Symanski?" asked Detective Hughes.

"Yes! Look, Mark and I are lovers. We planned this together," said Céline. Detectives Hughes and Freeman exchanged another look.

"I'm afraid your story doesn't really add up Miss Molyneux. You see, we've already interviewed Mr. Symanski and he told us some very interesting things about you," said Detective Freeman.

"What things?" asked Céline. Detective Hughes opened the file on the table.

"Mr. Symanski gave you the job at the bank 9 months ago. He took you under his wing and trained you. You tried to show your appreciation by coming onto him but he knocked you back. Despite that incident, he let you keep your job. He decided to give you another chance. And this is how you repay him," said Detective Freeman. Céline banged her fists on the table.

"He's lying. Mark and I are lovers!" said Céline.

Detective Hughes turned the page in his file. "We've also spoken to the other employees at the bank. Every single one of them provides Mr. Symanski with a glowing character reference. They say he's a great boss, a man of integrity, a stickler for the rules. And they all say he's very happily married," said Detective Freeman.

"No! Look, I'm telling you the truth," cried Céline. Detective Hughes closed his file.

"I'll tell you what I think Miss Molyneux. I think you're clutching at straws. You know you're going to prison, and you're trying to drag Mr. Symanski down with you. Is it because he knocked you back? You're probably not used to that, a pretty young girl like you," said Detective Hughes. Céline shook her head.

"No, Mark is involved. He's set me up," she said.

"Miss Molyneux, there isn't a shred of evidence against Mr. Symanski but there's a mountain of evidence against you. It was you who volunteered to lock up, it was you that allowed your accomplice through the bank doors, it was you that led him to the back and it was you that tied up your colleagues. Plus, you have incriminating evidence in your flat," said Detective Freeman.

Céline sank back into her seat, shell shocked. "May I have a cigarette?" she whispered. Detective Hughes reached into his jacket pocket and pulled out a packet of cigarettes. With shaking hands, Céline lit the cigarette and took one deep drag.

"Are you ready to talk now Miss Molyneux?" asked Detective Hughes. Céline looked him straight in the eye.

"I'm not saying another word until I have a lawyer," she said.

Detectives Hughes gave Céline a cold smile. "Interview terminated at 9pm," he stated. He switched off the recorder and got to his feet.

"Come with me Miss Molyneux," he said.

"Where are you taking me?" asked Céline.

"To read you your rights," he said.

Panoptic

Jennifer R Widrig

She pulled the shiny card from her wallet. She kept it behind the picture of her kids to make her stop and think before she bought something, but all it did was make her buy things for them. Handing it over to the clerk, she looked down at the little screen, waiting for it to ask for her signature. She didn't look up at all. Soon, the line appeared and she used the stylus to scrawl out her name. A few seconds and it was over. The clean, white plastic bag was in her hand and she was making her way out the door. She didn't look back, just in case.

Driving home, she passed rows of meticulous houses. When a light turned red, she gazed casually to the right and admired the feverishly green hop vine arching over a walkway. A For Sale sign was freshly planted in front. The house behind was painted in earth tones. It sat modestly back from the curb, a neat front porch with a wooden swing was tucked just behind a young maple tree. The light changed and she lurched forward. Her house was in the next block.

At home in front of her computer she typed in the address and checked the house's price. The monthly payment would be more than double her rent. Yet her house was nice. It was fairly new, with stainless steel appliances and those brown-black cabinets that reeked of modernity and efficiency. Anyone visiting might get the impression that they had remodeled it themselves. That they actually owned any of this.

Suddenly, a memory. She was in 7th grade, down at the corner store with her friends. They were buying burritos and mini-pizzas to microwave for their lunches. She didn't have any money, but she decided to get one, too. She told the clerk to put it on her parent's account, which they paid at the end of the month. When that day came, she watched her parents closely, waiting for them to say something about the charges. Would they be mad? Would she have to pay them back? But it seemed to pass without notice. A few months later she tried it again. Not too often, but about once a week by the end of the year. No mention was ever made of it.

In high school she had regularly taken money from her mother's purse. A dollar. Or five. If it was much more Mom tended to notice, would ask her father if he had borrowed it. But a dollar, even every day, wasn't noticed. It stuck her as oddly miraculous. How could they not know how much money they had at any given time?

In college it was the credit card her father had given her for emergencies. She used it for silly splurges. Fancy shoes, beautiful plates, a dinner out. They never mentioned it. She started to think she deserved it. Of course they wouldn't ask her to pay it! It was only a bit here and there. It didn't really add up to much. It wasn't worth mentioning.

The phone rang and she got up to answer it. It was her daughter's school, calling to remind them about the fundraising dinner on Saturday. She wasn't planning on going. She could barely pay the rent, how could she donate money to the school?

The elementary had seemed so quaint when they started there. The teachers were young and earnest; the kids sat at tables in groups instead of desks. She had liked that. Now it seemed like the school was always pinching at her, asking for money and time and donations. Sometimes she could barely focus to help her daughter with her schoolwork. The thought of the coming storm of bills and payments loomed so heavily in front of her.

When they had first gotten married, she had bought whatever they needed, no matter the price. Occasionally she would look for bargains, but ultimately, any savings she got she spent on other things. No longer shoes and fancy handbags, but durable, household items that would add to the image of the well-stocked home. She felt practical and far-sighted. These were things she could use the rest of her life.

But what good did they do her now? Yes, she had a beautiful cake plate and trifle dish. But she could no longer afford to make fancy desserts. Mostly, she tried to keep everyone fed as cheaply as possible. They all seemed to eat constantly, asking for something else as soon as they'd finished a meal. It was like when her children were babies, and nursed so long she felt like they were sucking the food out of her stomach.

She checked the clock. Soon her husband would be home with the kids and it would begin. She took a few minutes to make cup of tea and stretch out on the couch. They had bought the couch a few months before because the previous one had a big tear in the leather. It had started out as a tiny rip but gradually grew across the whole cushion. She couldn't bear the sight of it.

She started to plan dinner. There was a chicken recipe from a cooking show she liked that she was going to try. A new recipe always made her feel so happy, like a painter before a blank canvas. She ran through a mental list of what else could go with the chicken and settled on baked beans. She found them disgustingly sweet and mushy, but the rest of the family seemed to like them.

One night, a few years back, she had been drifting off to sleep, thinking about the bills. The credit card bills started to add themselves up in her head. Her eyes had jerked open and her chest began to pound. A pulse of panic shot down to the end of her fingertips. How had it happened? How had she spent so much? She resolved to stop spending. To only buy what she could pay for from her checking account. The "cash only" system, they called it. But then there was that embarrassing scene in the grocery store, when her debit card had been rejected for lack of funds. Not enough money to buy the week's groceries? Her face grew hot now, thinking about it. So now if she was even a bit unsure whether there was enough in the account, she would charge it. The credit card was never rejected. She had been given a limit large enough to buy a luxury car, for God's sake.

She would go through periods when she was very disciplined with herself. Drove past all the restaurants and gourmet grocery shops without a flinch. Then there would be a necessity, something it seemed ridiculous to do without. And there she would be at a huge, well-lit store with glimmering white aisles, and everything would look like a necessity. Or too good a bargain to pass up. She felt like an alcoholic, but without a sponsor to call. She expected that, at any moment, someone would stop her. A stranger perhaps. They would step up to her cart and say, "What are you doing? Put all this back." But everyone seemed to want her to buy more. They would so politely step out of the way for her and her cart. They would grab things from top shelves that she couldn't reach. "There you go" they'd say, smiling.

And here she was. Drowning. Invisibly. It seemed like only a matter of time before she would go under completely. What that looked like, even she didn't know. Would they come to the door and knock politely? Or would they take her away roughly, in handcuffs, shaking their heads in sheer disbelief. How could someone so smart be such a fool?

She was educated after all. She and her husband had professional degrees. So how come they couldn't make it work? They had never thought much about paying off their student loans. They payed the amount they were asked every month, after all. But here they were, 15 years out of college and still paying back the damn loans. She wondered if they would pay them off before the children were in college themselves.

She got up and dumped out the cold tea left in her cup. Thought again about what to make for dinner. Chicken. That's right. She would get it out so it could warm up. And beans. She put the turquoise can on the counter. It made a metallic clink as it hit the marble. She put the can opener next to it.

She saw the mailbox outside and headed out to check it. There was a movie she didn't remember putting in her queue. The cable bill. Checks from one of the credit card companies, encouraging her to take a romantic getaway or fix up the house. She tossed it all on the table and went upstairs to sort the laundry.

As she was going through the pockets of her husband's pants, she felt a small, soft piece of paper. It was money. Cash. She looked at it in her hand. All the intricate details of the drawings and numbers. The nubbly outline of the number in the corner was pressing into her thumb. She sat down on the floor and smoothed it out on her knee. She pressed it down, over and over, trying to make it lay flat. Suddenly she thought of the white bag she had brought home. That had cost exactly what this bill was. Exactly the amount she had put on her credit card.

She started to laugh, then her face crinkled, her eyes seemed to squeeze themselves shut. Hot tears dropped onto the bill in her lap. The squeezing moved to her chest and she gasped, laughing and crying and pushing her face into the floor. Her pulse rushed into her lowered head and swished in her ears like the wings of a horrid bird.

And then the swishing was voices, movement, people all around her. There were people on the stairs and outside the house, trying to see in, knocking on the doors and windows. Asking for the money. They knocked and then pounded, the steady rapping, rapping of their grabbing pink hands. They pulled at her clothes, her neck. She wasn't going to let them have it. She wasn't going to.

She crinkled up the bill, smashing it down, smaller and smaller, as small as it would go, and stuffed it into her mouth. Swallowed.

It was over. They had gone. She was alone on the floor of the silent hallway. She wiped the tears from her face and stood up. She went downstairs to make dinner.

Will You Miss Me?

Third Prize Winner
Jack Noble

Ellie's been letting herself go. Look at her - she wobbles.

"You know, you wobble a bit these days." She's moving things around the kitchen, taking things from here and putting them over there.

"Only when I move," she says. "You should try that. Moving, I mean."

I take a sip of wine. "Maybe if you moved a little faster you wouldn't wobble quite so much. Like round a running track once or twice a week."

She doesn't look at me. Busy moving those things, from here to there. "Like you, you mean? Been running lately?"

"Look at my svelte figure, woman. Don't need to run. I go easy on the chocolate cakes."

"Well, chocolate cakes are my consolation for not getting pissed every night."

I take an ostentatious gulp of wine but she's still not looking at me. "Are you casting aspersions?"

"Warnings, not aspersions. Alcoholism is boring."

"You find me boring now?"

"What do you mean, 'now'?"

And so on.

I want out. It's not that I no longer care for her. But when I dim the bathroom light and turn slightly to the left, the mirror shows me that I've still got it. A quick wit, too. Bitingly funny and handsome as hell. I'm depriving womanhood by sticking to my vows. So I've come up with a plan: take off my wedding ring and drive around the country for a couple of months. Turn up in small towns pretending to be a single writer on the hunt for inspiration. Nail all the young small town girls I neglected to nail when I was young myself.

New neighbours are moving in. Young. Newlyweds? Unlikely, unless that four year old boy is someone's little brother. Boxes on the lawn. Removal men do the heavy work. The new neighbours run in and out of the house, laughing excitedly. They seem overjoyed to be here. Here! On Rosebank Avenue. Well, I suppose the sun is shining this morning. They're probably telling each other that it's a 'good omen', that it 'bodes well' and so forth. She's a shapely young thing. Irritating voice, though. Like a chipmunk from that movie. He clearly adores her, today, on this auspicious summer morning. And why not? I'm half-way to adoring her myself. But that figure will soon change and that voice will stay just the same.

"You used to laugh at my jokes."

"They used to be funny."

"But they're the same jokes."

"Really? Maybe it's me that's changed, then. Ten years is a long time."

"That's never ten years, is it?"

"Happy anniversary to you, too."

"Come here! Come here and see this!"

I find Ellie in the living room looking out the window. She is wearing a sweet smile that can't possibly be for me. The boy is running around the neighbours' garden absorbed in some military fantasy.

"Oh, it's a child playing next door. I thought we'd won the lottery or something."

"No, dear. Seems it's the neighbours who won the lottery."

We watch him play.

"Look at his self-absorption. How I envy it. I need at least half a bottle to achieve that level of interest in anything."

"Do you think his parents are watching him, too?" She sounds dreamy. "Or are they used to it?"

"I imagine his parents are walking around in a permanent state of exhaustion. Probably not conscious enough to be described as 'watching' anything."

"Look how serious his expression is! Ha! Such a vivid imagination."

"Shame it won't last. Mine didn't."

"It's as if he can actually see other people there with him."

"Yeah. Kids don't get lonely. That comes later."

"His parents must be so happy."

"Must they?"

She looks at me with what appears to be a sad kind of love. "You were like a little boy when we first met," she said. "So playful."

"I'm still playful," I say; and then I'm lost for words. My instinct is to tell her how beautiful she looks when she's not bitching at me. I used to say things like that to her; but those were the old days. Repetition dulls, doesn't it? You say something meaningful too often and the words lose their power. So you stop saying it. The future is silence.

"Why did you have to grow up?" She's still smiling sadly. I imagine her smiling like that while saying 'It was a wonderful service. He would have liked it.' I look away.

"It's only my body that's old. Oh, and my mind. And not forgetting my soul. Everything else remains bright-eyed and innocent."

"I'm thinking of quitting my job. Taking a couple of months off."

"Really? You want to devote more time to drinking?"

"Well you know how cool I look nursing a glass of red."

"Sure. It really sets off your eyes."

"Nice. Anyway."

"What will you do? A little more housework, presumably."

"I wouldn't dream of trespassing. Actually I thought I might take a trip. You know, I've seen the Pyramids, and the Great Wall of China. But there are a lot of places in Britain I've never visited."

"Really? There can't be many pubs you haven't been to."

The neighbours hold a house warming party. Guests sweep in the front and out into the back garden. We can hear their conversations through our open window. I attempt to watch '24' on DVD but the goings on next door are too distracting so I turn it off. Ellie looks up from her book.

"No glass of wine tonight?"

I indicate next door. "I wasn't invited."

"I'll have one with you."

I pour two glasses of white. I sit on the sofa and Ellie sits on the armchair opposite.

"Are you serious about taking that trip?"

"Sure."

She looks at her glass. "I'm not invited?"

"Well, sure, it's just your work - you know. You want to come?"

"No, you're right, I have to work. It's just that, we haven't been travelling together for three years."

"Well. After China, you said you couldn't stand to meet any more American tourists."

A smile. "Remember the one who expressed surprise that the Great Wall had stood for so long without being blown down by the wind?"

"Ha! That was the highlight of the whole trip."

Laughter from the neighbours' garden. I mentally categorise the new neighbours and their friends as 'laugh-easily' types. Which means Ellie and I will probably get on well enough with them without ever becoming close friends. Suits me. If they were friends, they would always be calling round, wouldn't they?

I realise we have both been staring into our glasses. I have the sudden urge to get up and hug Ellie. But spontaneous hugs are out of fashion in our house. Instead I ask, "Have you met them yet? The neighbours."

"Briefly. They seem happy. I welcomed them to the street. But somehow it felt like it was them who ought to be welcoming me."

"You say the smartest things. Pity no-one but me is smart enough to understand you."

Old joke. Smile response achieved. Urge to hug subdued, if not completely extinguished.

I turn '24' back on.

After a few minutes Ellie joins me on the sofa and we clink glasses. "Poor Jack Bauer," she says.

"Poor Jack?"

"Sure. I know you want to be him, but –"

"I *am* him, darling."

" Right... I know you want to be him, but really – his life is a constant misery."

"Told you I was him."

I put my arm around her, and watch Jack Bauer as he struggles to resolve yet another impossible dilemma.

I like to make Ellie laugh in the morning. Morning is like Halloween – it's the time of day when we're most vulnerable to evil spirits. The sound of Ellie's laughter frightens them away.

"Damn. Forgot to get coffee." I throw the newspaper across the table. "Scan this for good news, would you? I'd do it myself but I have to drive to work in ten minutes and I don't want to be blinded by tears. Might cause an accident."

"Ha. You can cry when you get there."

"Yeah. As usual."

Ellie jabs at the front page with her finger. "Hey, you're not going to believe this, but I found something positive already. It seems the government's new mission is to make the nation happier."

"What? Wasn't that always their mission?"

"I guess not."

"Well, well. That explains everything."

She reads. "'The prime minister said: 'It's time we admitted that there's more to life than money and it's time we focused not just on GDP but on GWB – general wellbeing.'"

"Good Lord. This is wonderful news. Hey, what time does the post usually get here?"

"Eight thirty. You expecting something?"

"Package from the prime minister."

"Our happiness allowance?"

"Absolutely! A crate of pinot noir for me and a little bundle of joy for you."

I regret saying it even before I finish the sentence. Maybe even before I started saying it. Ellie doesn't look up from the newspaper, nor does her smile falter. But her silence is eloquent. Somewhere in my mind the evil spirits of morning concoct a potentially catastrophic joke about a pregnant silence, but my prefrontal cortex mounts a sabotage operation before it can be deployed. I experience a familiar sinking feeling in my stomach. Once again I've failed in my simple marital duty to keep my wife in good spirits. It occurs to me to apologise but I dismiss the idea. An apology would merely confirm that the issue is real. And we don't want that. Not with a day of work ahead and no coffee in the house.

I get up and kiss the top of her head.

"Have a lovely day, gorgeous." She mumbles something, touches my hand, tries to smile. As I leave the house I'm thinking that in twelve years together we've never had a real argument, with raised voices and saying terrible things in the heat of the moment and all that. And that has nothing to do with me, and everything to do with her.

The skies open in the evening, just as I arrive home. Dinner is subdued. The rain hammers against the kitchen window. I don't know if she's still thinking about what I said this morning. Maybe she's forgotten all about it. But I haven't. My sense of failure imbues everything. The house seems small (because I never became rich). My body seems frail (because I never joined a gym). My chicken stir-fry seems bland (because the first time I cooked for her I was a novice chef and years later, I still am).

I want out.

After dinner Ellie suggests a glass of wine. I raise my eyebrows.

"Are you turning into me? Maybe I should get stuck into the chocolate cakes."

"Well, this might be the last evening we spend together for a while."

"It might?"

"Aren't you going on a trip?"

"Yes, but I hadn't decided when."

"Really? All through dinner you had this 'I just can't take any more' expression on your face. So I assumed you'd be leaving this weekend."

She is acting as if this is all perfectly okay with her. Is it? Can that be true?

"Maybe you're right. Maybe I should go tomorrow."

She smiles broadly. I can't see any hurt or anxiety in that smile at all. After twelve years, can she still hide things from me?

"What will you do when I'm gone?"

"Oh, go to a lot of parties I suppose."

"Really? You've never been to a party in your life."

"No need! Living with you is like a constant party."

"Right. A funeral party."

She laughs, and I know at least that her laughter is genuine, if not unambiguously happy.

I get up early while Ellie is still asleep. The rain is on again. Not good weather for driving.

I feel excited about getting away. A growing sense of freedom. Underneath this, a tiny doubt. Guilt. Should I be leaving Ellie like this? But she is not a child. And although she would never say it, she needs time away from me, too.

I pack a bag in five minutes, enjoying the ritual and also the fact of its brevity, feeling that old male pride: I have no chains that cannot be conveniently cast aside when desired.

After a quick breakfast I grab an umbrella and take my bag out to the car, planning to return to the house to say goodbye to Ellie. I get into the driver's seat to check the car for litter.

Commotion at the door of the neighbours' house catches my attention.

The young man, wearing a tracksuit, is standing on his doorstep yelling into the house. A moment later he takes a step back as his beautiful wife appears in the doorway. Now he is standing unprotected under the merciless onslaught of the rain. After two seconds of that he has all the apparent dignity of a wet dog barking on a lawn. His wife, dressed in a silk dressing gown, keeps her eyes lowered as she slowly shuts the door.

He stops shouting and stares at the door for a moment. Then he looks up, and as if suddenly realising that it's raining, makes a dash for his car.

His car is parked on his driveway, which is no more than spitting distance from mine. I look at him through the rain streaming down our respective side windows. He sits motionless. After a moment, and without a clear motive, I beep my horn and he looks round. I give a friendly wave. He raises a tentative hand in reply. I wind down my window a little and after a short pause he does the same thing. He looks at me expectantly.

"Hi!" I have to yell against the sound of the rain. "I'm Gus. We're neighbours!"

"Ian. Nice to meet you." He nods, which is polite enough for me. I'm hardly expecting a smile.

"Hell of a morning, isn't it?"

"Terrible. Miserable weather." He speaks distractedly, as if simultaneously trying to think of a way out of the conversation.

I persevere. "And it's been so beautiful lately."

"Yes, hasn't it?" He seems more enthusiastic about the subject now, as if I've expressed a startling insight. "My wife and I moved in on Monday. We were saying then how gorgeous it was. Funny, how quickly it can change."

Not really. That's British weather, isn't it? People say the stupidest things when forced to make small talk.

"Indeed it is," I say. "You must have thought it was a good omen."

He looks me in the eye for the first time. "You know, that's exactly what we said."

"It's all gone wrong now, though, has it?"

"Excuse me?"

"Well, a blissful future begins on Monday, and a disastrous argument ends it on Saturday."

"Oh, yes, I see. You heard all that then, did you?"

"Not really. But it looked like the midpoint in a romantic

comedy."

"Ha. Right. But that's good, that means things will get better. Doesn't it?" He looks at me hopefully.

"Well, life ain't like the movies, mate." He looks genuinely crestfallen, as if what I say carries some authority. >From where did I obtain this sudden power? Does he think I have a crystal ball on the dashboard? I feel obliged to say something encouraging. "I think the rain might be easing off. Could be a good omen." The end of this last sentence is obliterated by a roar of thunder. Seems my crystal ball is faulty. I try a different tack.

"I saw you guys moving in. You looked like such a happy family. Made me feel envious."

His interest is piqued. "Oh yeah?"

"Sure. I can just tell you two are made for each other."

"Well." He's facing forward, towards his house. "I thought you said life aint like the movies."

"Forget the movies. And you have a beautiful little boy. Some people would give their right arm for what you've got."

He seems a little embarrassed now. What did I expect? Well, that my inspirational words would send him striding purposefully back to the house, I suppose. But after all, I don't know what they were arguing about, do I? For all I know, Ian's been whipping his son with a power cord. The police could be on their way.

This is none of my business. I better get out of here.

But Ian speaks. "You're right, you know. We are made for each other. And my son is the most beautiful boy in the world."

It's my turn to squirm. He's not looking at me, so I amuse

myself by pretending to puke over my lap.

"These arguments," he goes on. "They're just so stupid. I'm sitting out here in my car when I should be in there with them."

A response seems in order, so I say: "Absolutely!"

He turns to me. "Thanks for the chat, Gus. I'll catch you later."

"Sure. Uh, later then."

He smiles and nods, winds up the window, climbs out of the car and strides purposefully back to his house. He finds the door locked and bangs on it, shouting, for a good three minutes before he is let in.

"Go get 'em, tiger," I say.

It occurs to me that I don't believe in the possibility of an enduring happiness. I live for good moments, and this is one of them: an amusing encounter behind me and a promising vacation ahead. And in the meantime, I have a nice little anecdote for Ellie. As I head back to the house, I consider how best to relate the episode. Hopefully she's still asleep so I can wake her up to hear it. There's nothing I like more in the world, than to make Ellie laugh in the morning.

毛延寿

Mao Yanshou

Second Prize Winner
Diane Ward

1

有錢能使鬼推磨

(If you have money you can make the devil push your grindstone.)

Mao Yanshou studied the girl from the Wang family as apathetically as if he were inspecting livestock. The mother of the family was busy serving him the crude food of the Zigui village, while murmuring hopeful compliments about her daughter. Across the cramped candlelit room, the father stood rigid, anxious for Yanshou's approval.

Yanshou nodded his head in thanks to the mother for the meal, although he had no intention of eating the villager's food.

With growing unease, he looked back to their daughter.

A pit of budding dread had begun to form in his stomach. It was impossible, he thought, for her to actually have been born to these parents. The parents of the Wang family - while not completely unattractive - were far from the standards of beauty in the Chang'an palace. They had dark skin from working long hours in the sun, and rough calloused hands that would be considered barbaric among nobility.

Due to his eye for beauty as the court's artist, the emperor had sent Mao Yanshou to tour the Han country to find and bring back more acceptable girls to add to his harem. At first he had detested the idea and complied bitterly, hating to leave the luxuries of court for the dirt floors and single roomed houses of the country. The only redemption he had found was that it was marginally profitable to coax bribes from the families by promising that their daughters would find favor in the emperor's court only to "regrettably" inform them afterwards that the harem could no longer accept anyone else. Yanshou had by now sent back hundreds of hopeful concubines to the harem and dismissed at least twice as many.

As the emperor's harem swelled in number, it had grown customary that the emperor no longer viewed the actual girls, but instead chose his favorites by Yanshou's portraits which he could look through quickly. Yanshou had instantly seen a way to exploit these girls and their families by demanding bribes in exchange for a pleasing portrait.

But this girl from the rural village, she was too beautiful.

Her family would think they didn't need to pay him his customary amount since her natural beauty would be sufficient. That thought troubled him more than it should have, and he found himself deeply resentful that he had journeyed here to their mist filled cesspool for nothing.

The Wang family stared at him with eyes like starving animals waiting to be thrown a scrap.

Yanshou's mood worsened with every minute that slipped away until finally the girl and her mother excused themselves and the father stood waiting uneasily for Yanshou's discernment. Yanshou hated to watch the man. He hated the pathetic look on the man's face. For a moment he entertained the idea of kicking the man back as he would a dog.

But Yanshou only inclined his head slightly in a bow, before remarking that he was fatigued and would think on what he observed today. As the family left the room, he tried furiously to think of how he may still profit from these people with the unnaturally exquisite girl.

2

无事不怕鬼叫门

(If you've done nothing wrong, you shouldn't worry about devils knocking on your door at midnight.)

An opaque mist had seeped into the Zigui village.

When Mao Yanshou had ridden in on the entourage from the Chang'an palace yesterday, he had thought nothing of it. But as he prolonged his stay here, the mist had thickened and seemed to even be leaking into the houses.

The Wang family, whose house was only two rooms, had offered him their main room while the rest of the entourage from the palace lodged outside. Even though it was well into the night,

Yanshou found the thin bed uncomfortable. He paced irritably as he considered how he could profit from this pitiable visit.

Once he tired from pacing the small room, Yanshou came to the window and watched the odd sight forming outside. As he looked out on the mist, he considered the deeply striking Wang girl.

Yanshou remembered what the mother had murmured to him as she served his food, "She washes her hands in the river every day and it makes her beautiful." The girl's faultless face troubled him. He had heard far too many tales of the occult - spirits rising up and drowning men.

The Xiangxi River's mist, which welled near the edge of Zigui, seemed to be moving on its own as if there was an otherworldly wind blowing it. Even though he could only barely see the river from here, he imagined it as a deathly still, murky pool with too dark water that glistened enticingly.

"Water yaogui," he mumbled to himself, recalling the childhood stories he had listened to about the lithe, mysterious creatures that slept on the bottom of rivers. What it would mean to wash one's hands in a yaogui's river he didn't know; however, he couldn't help but imagine that as the girl dipped her hands into the river, it was the spirit's tongue that licked her hands clean.

Yanshou stood by the window unable to sleep for the rest of the night.

The river seemed to be dripping out its presence through the mist, soaking the residents with its influence.

3

人心不足蛇吞象

(A man's greed is like a snake that wants to swallow an elephant.)

The following morning Yanshou managed to convince the Wang family to pay a bribe. Unfortunately they were too poor to pay him at the moment, but they promised that once she made it to the palace she would have his money and give it to him when he was to paint her portrait. Yanshou was annoyed at the delay, but he was certain the emperor would praise him for finding such a beautiful creature, so he let it slide while telling himself he was far too generous.

Yanshou left Zigui and continued traveling Han country, visiting various villages and collecting bribes from hopeful families only to reject their daughters in the end. His pockets swelled and the Wang girl receded to the back of his mind.

When he returned to the Chang'an palace, he found a mist had risen up near the palace gates. It reminded him vividly of the mist that had surrounded Zigui and a familiar terror threatened to grow up in him. Yanshou insisted on avoiding the mist and made the entourage camp outside the palace.

After the mist dissipated, Yanshou cautiously returned to his lavish room in the Han palace. The floor was sticky with water from the mist and his skin rose into chill bumps even though the room was temperate. As the servants brought his new spoils to his already sumptuous room, he stood immobile staring outside.

He could see from his window someone playing a Han lute in the garden. Though he could barely see the figure, he recognized the deftly played folk melody which he had frequently heard in

Zigui. The girl from the Wang family plucked at the strings as the other initiate concubines stood nearby.

She's brought the yaogui with her in the mist, he thought with disbelieving horror, and then in the next moment rejected this as nonsense. It was impossible for the Xiangxi's mist to have followed her here!

Yanshou soon resumed his task of painting the girls and again his purse was bloated beyond what it could hold from the bribes alone, excluding his pay from the emperor. But despite his good fortune, he was shaken and had been unable to sleep. He sat at his window every night waiting to see if the mist would creep in. It had settled in his mind that if he were to fall asleep it may seep in at night and spiral down his throat and choke him.

At work he painted the initiate concubines with ease. By countless repetition his long, lithe fingers could paint their simple faces with elegant perfection with little thought. He rarely even looked at the girls anymore and instead painted the same face over and over with minor changes depending on how much they had given him. A less talented or experienced artist's paintings may have suffered from the insomnia, but to him the job was the easiest of tasks.

The days swam together. Faces after nameless faces unimportant among the emperor's thousands flowed through his studio like the money that flowed to his purse. And at night he stood still by his window like as a statue, unable to rest.

It wasn't until one of the girls did not offer to pay his bribe that he was he shaken out of the blur. He had held out his hand expectantly without even lifting his eyes from his brush when he was met only with silence.

Raising his eyes from the clean, expectant parchment, he

gazed at the girl from the remote Zigui village that washed her hands in the Xiangxi river. He could smell the water on her---its alluring, enticing fragrance.

His moment of alarm was replaced with practiced disdain that had become too habitual for him to even be aware of it.

His tired eyes ached to look at her. She had a face beyond perfection, so excruciatingly beautiful that he could never have even claim to have painted a creature so blemishless. Her only fault, which yet did not even diminish her beauty, was that one shoulder sloped slightly more than the other and it was something only one with a knowing eye could see.

"You bring me nothing?" he asked tersely, his tongue feeling swollen in his mouth and as tired as his eyes.

She politely bowed her head in agreement. It was maddening how demurely and innocently she was able to concede this. Yanshou felt as if someone had rammed a pole into his chest, trying to shove out his pride. No one had ever denied him. Indignation replaced the watery dread that had settled in his core.

Turning back to the blank page in renewed vigor, he painted a portrait not of her face but a reflection of his indignation.

It was the most hideous portrait he had ever painted. The painting was of a sour faced girl with life-stripped eyes overshadowed by an oppressive brow and ruddy skin. A vengeful feeling of self accomplishment swelled in him as he handed the portrait to the servant to be hung out to dry and then given to the emperor.

4

滴水穿石

(Dripping water can eat through a stone.)

Years had passed since Mao Yanshou had painted the unrightfully repulsive portrait of the Wang girl.

The wind hissed, causing his hair to sting his eyes. He could not feel his hands because they were so tightly tied to two poles as he awaited his execution.

He whispered curses for the beautiful girl and his own actions. He had already shed all the tears he could. His mouth felt dry and his skin was burned and cracked from the sun. This wasn't worth the sum of money so small and inconsequential that he had requested before.

He relived his downfall as he waited for his death.

The Xiongnu barbarian king of the large southern nomadic tribe had wanted a bride from the Han Empire to seal a peace treaty. In concordance the emperor decided to wed one of his concubines to the barbarian leader. When the Wang girl and two other concubines volunteered the emperor surveyed their portraits and thought nothing of giving any of the plain girls, least of all the one from the Wang family. The emperor felt he had triumphed in a small way, outwitting the barbarian king.

How Yanshou had rejoiced to hear this! After all it would remove all chances of the emperor discovering the deception of the Wang girl's portrait. But more importantly to him, maybe then the awful mist that plagued his nightmares would go with her and he would finally be able to live freely again.

Unsurprisingly to Yanshou, the barbarian king had chosen her out of the three and they were to depart in only a matter of days.

It was as if a physical weight had been lifted from him, as if the yaogui's mist had somehow weighed him down and now was finally starting to drift away.

It wasn't until the day before they were to depart that the Xiongnu sent an envoy to the emperor. The Xiongnu's envoy had graciously thanked the emperor for the great beauty he had gifted them, and for her exquisite talent and elegant bearing, saying that the Xiongnu king took this generous gesture as a sign of a lasting peace between them.

The emperor had been astonished.

He had commanded that the Wang's girl portrait be found and was amazed to find it so blatantly contradictory to the Xiongnu king's depiction.

Suspicious of the portrait's truth, the emperor invited the Xiongnu king and his bride to appear in court for a farewell feast before they departed from the city. It had only taken a glance for the emperor to determine the deception. He became furious, knowing he could not retract his word, and knowing that he would lose his most beautiful and talented concubine because of Yanshou.

Yanshou was oblivious to the events until the imperial guards apprehended him. The emperor had commanded that Yanshou not be allowed to attend the feast, as he was already suspicious that the deception had come from Yanshou. Before the feast had even ended, Yanshou was seized in his studio and imprisoned. The following day he was condemned to execution for his deception. It wasn't until after he had been condemned that he realized where he had been undone.

The beautiful girl.

The utter improbability of the events amazed him. It was as if the gods had conspired against him. With cracked lips, he sobbed dryly and quietly. There was nothing worse than this helpless rage knowing how close he was to being executed.

The wind blew strong and cold at his back with an unsettling dampness to it.

Yanshou gritted his teeth at the thought that a storm may blow in.

Why should that small sum of money be worth this? he wondered.

A light rain started to fall and the water felt like thousands of fallings needles to his burned skin. He saw the faces of the villagers staring at him in the mist as they had before when he rode into the Zigui Village. As if they had known.

"Curse you all," Yanshou spat angrily. His voice broke as he tried to yell "I asked only for a small amount. I murdered no one. I do not deserve this..." But it came as only a slurred murmuring as his tongue remained like stone in his mouth.

He could vaguely see mist swirling at his feet and climbing the shallow stairs towards him. Whether it was a hallucination or not, mattered nothing to him now as panic gripped him.

After the rain, another opaque mist rolled into the village and covered the center where Yanshou was bound. The emperor had intended to leave the corpse to overlook the village as a warning, but when the mist peeled away, the body was gone.

Where There's a Will

First Prize Winner
Leo Madigan

The phone rang in the office of Saples & Saples, Solicitors, Queen Street, Auckland. Julia answered it. Her face clouded. "I'll be right over." she said.

"Who's died?" asked a colleague.

"Quintus Kirkwood. The maid found him in his kitchen. Peaceful and painless apparently."

"Wow! All that money. Is there a will?"

"It's sealed in a bank. Cancel my engagements indefinitely." She took up her brief-case and made for the door. "I'm the executor," she said.

Julia crossed town. Quintus Kirkwood's apartment was unostentatious; it had none of the extras associated with wealth. But that was in character. Quintus, for all his genius on the world's stock markets had been a quiet, modest man, avuncular, even with peers. He had never married yet was always at ease with women and children. It was said that in his youth he had applied to join the Franciscan brotherhood, but there was no one to confirm that.

The body was laid out in the bedroom, a placid smile still evident around the corners of the lifeless mouth. The undertakers had left saying they would be back in an hour with transport.

Julia went directly to the cabinet in Quintus' office. There was a file marked *Final Briefing* which Quintus had pointed out to her on several occasions. In it was an envelope with the words, *To be opened, gently, on my demise.* Julia chuckled at the word 'gently'. Typical Quintus.

As his solicitor, Julia was familiar with the Kirkwood business transactions but she had never been made privy to the beneficiaries or terms of his will. Quintus hadn't actually been secretive, though when she had made a diplomatic enquiry he had winked and said, "Good heavens, woman! I must be discreet. You might be a beneficiary yourself."

Quintus couldn't be blamed if he saw no satisfactory future for the money he had accumulated falling into the hands of his sister and her feral brood down Wellington way. Julia had met them once – her married name was Blake – and had been appalled at their vulgarity, their avarice. She suspected that Quintus kept them in the colonial mansion he owned on Mount Victoria to prevent them from squatting on his doorstep.

The envelope contained a note addressed to Julia, along with an authority and password for the bank vault. The note was explicit. She was to personally inform his old friend Father Keenan of his death, and Father Keenan was to tell his sister. She was one of his parishioners in St Margaret's, Wellington, though she had probably never set foot across the church threshold. Quintus made it clear that he wanted to be buried from St. Margaret's, but there must be no fuss. Both Julia and Father Keenan were asked to release details of the requiem and burial only to those who specifically asked. However, Quintus had added, she could make the reading of the will as public as she wished. She could hire the Auckland Town Hall if she wanted or get a slot on the television news because, he hinted mischievously, there might be surprises.

***

Fr. Pat Keenan had just finished conducting a wedding when Julia phoned. A heart attack, she had said, to be confirmed by autopsy. The priest was stunned momentarily. Quintus and he were the same age, 67; they were from the same streets, had attended the same schools, played in the same teams. Quintus, who had been struggling with his thesis at the time of Pat's ordination, had hitch-hiked the 400 miles from Auckland to Wellington to attend the ceremony.

Years later, when he had been appointed parish priest of St. Margaret's and Quintus was listed not too far below oil princes and media magnates on the 'world's most wealthy' lists, funds for parish projects would materialize from a seemingly invisible source.

Quintus, too, had bought Howick House, a colonial mansion overlooking the harbour, not 5 minutes stroll from the church. He had intended to live there himself but had offered it to his sister as a temporary home when she married. Mavis Blake and her issue had ignored the temporariness of the arrangement for 30 years.

Quintus had visited Fr. Keenan in May and presented him with a large, elegantly bound book chained to a waist-high lectern carved from *kohekohe*, a native mahogany. The pages were blank. "A sort of social registry," Quintus had explained. "Those who attend weddings, baptisms, funerals sign their names. Historians ten generations hence will thank you. It also makes signees feel they have a personal stake in the institution. Churches in Corsica swear by it."

***

Fr. Keenen shook himself out of his reverie. He said a *De Profundis* for the soul of his friend and resolved to offer a novena of Masses. He then prepared to call on Mavis Blake to break the news of her brother's death.

From the road there was little indication that behind the unruly hedge lay grounds and gardens and a splendid palladian bungalow. There was a cattle-grid at the entrance to the driveway. After some yards the driveway was lost behind huge macrocarpas, standing like golden guards before the lair of some giant ogre.

A young Maori wearing only khaki shorts was steering a mower over the acre of lawn in front of the house. Fr. Keenan waved in greeting and called, "Hi!" The young man was surprised to be acknowledged. He smiled but made no answer. Perhaps he was shy. Or perhaps he was afraid of the woman striding up the gravel path from the tennis courts.

When he was nearer, Fr. Keenan greeted the woman. She paused and raised a hand to shield her eyes. "Oh, you!" she muttered and dropped her hand. "If you're collecting you've come to the wrong window."

Fr. Keenan said gently, "I'm afraid, Mrs Blake, that I'm the bearer of sad news."

She was a big woman, short on finesse. "Mrs Blake, now, huh?

It's *that bloody Mavis* behind my back."

"You brother died this morning of a heart attack. It was quick and peaceful by all accounts."

Mavis went rigid. The whine of the motor-mower cut out and the young man called, "I've finished here Mrs Blake. I can't do the courts because they're being used."

She turned towards the courts and shouted, "Get up here right away. Your uncle's snuffed it." A brusque jolt of her head told the gardener that the courts would now be clear to mow. "I hope he had sense to leave the house to me," she muttered. "What about the money? Who's going to get the money?"

She ignored Fr. Keenan and turned towards the house. Then, as an afterthought she asked the priest, "What are the arrangements?"

"The funeral date will be set after the autopsy."

"And the will? Where's the will?"

"Apparently there will be a public reading in Auckland around the same time."

***

The newspapers were full of the Kirkwood death. Tributes came from all over. Wall Street and the Bourse observed 5 seconds silence in respect for the passing. The autopsy confirmed the heart attack and the funeral was arranged with Fr. Keenan according to the wishes of the deceased. It coincided with the Memorial service to be held in Auckland Cathedral, prior to a much trumpeted reading of the will.

Speculation ran high. Waiters and hotel doormen told of Quintus's gratuities, charities told of flash finances from the same source. The local papers gnawed all revelations to the bone. The name of Quintus Kirkwood became synonymous with lavish and eccentric generosity.

***

Hemi Harris saw Fr. Keenan in Courteney Place. He was with fellow university students when the priest, walking passed, recognised him as the lawn-keeper at Howick House and said "Hi!" Hemi turned back and joined him. They walked some yards together.

"What was that about?" his companions asked when he returned. Hemi wasn't too communicative, but he did say that he was enquiring about a funeral of someone he worked for. That was all. To have mentioned Quintus might have suggested claims of associating with the rich and famous.

Hemi had tended the lawns at Howick House since he was 10. He had little regard for the Blakes who spoke to their dogs with more respect than they spoke to him. However, on the rare occasions that Mr. Kirkwood visited, the great man had sought out Hemi and lifted the boy's self esteem with his gracious manner. And when Mr. Kirkwood learned that Hemi's payment was erratic, and often inaccurate, he set up an account for him with regular payment and regular increments. These had been forthcoming ever since. No way was that the work of the Blakes.

Hemi suddenly turned again and ran after Fr. Keenan. "Padre!" he called. "Vicar!" He wasn't sure how a Catholic priest should be addressed. "Can anyone go to the funeral? I mean, like, does a fella have to be a Catholic."

Fr. Keenan couldn't restrain a chuckle. "Doors wide open," he said and added, "What's your name?" Hemi told him. Fr. Keenan introduced himself and explained where St. Margaret's church stood.

***

Speculation about Quintus' will had become an overnight industry. An astrologer in Wanganui had worked out that the fortune was to provide free beer for all Kiwi nationals until either the supply or the money ran out. A Baltimore businessman who knew Quintus well swore that Quintus had told him his billions would be used to establish a foundation for the education of orphans. A soothsayer claimed divine enlightenment when disclosing that the money would fund an award comparable to the Nobel Prize, for plumbers, butchers and rugby players. Oh yes, the days preceding the reading were carnival time for the media.

No political rally or movie premiere had drawn such crowds to tv screens on the morning set aside for the reading. Monitors were erected in the inner city and a parade organized down Queen Street to lay flowers on a waterfront monument hastily erected to honour the great financier.

Excitement verged on delirium as the highpoint approached. Julia, on the studio rostrum with lenses and lights focused on her, gave a key to the mayor. The mayor opened a small strong-box on the table in front of him. He lifted the lid, took out a document and handed it to Julia.

Julia Saples adjusted her glasses and began to read.

Respectable bequests were made to individuals and organizations. Some stock here, some bonds there, all worthy and admirable. Then came the simple, unqualified statement, *The rest of my estate, all stocks and shares, investments, bullion, bank assets, properties etc, is to be divided equally among those attending my funeral at St Margaret's parish church in Wellington.*

At that very moment, Fr. Pat Keenan was closing the record book that Quintus had donated and returning it, and its lectern, to their corner in St. Margaret's sacristy. The only person who had signed it that morning was the solitary mourner at the Kirkwood funeral, the young Maori student who tended the lawns at Howick House.

Hemi had gone straight to Howick House from the Karori cemetery. He was late for work but it didn't matter because the Blakes, like everyone else in the world, were in Auckland for the reading of the Kirkwood will.

The Authors

Our winning author, **Leo Madigan,** was born in Nelson, New Zealand, during WWII and attended various schools around the islands. When he was 16 he went to sea on the British ships and spent most of the next 20 years on them. It was a delightful life, and a great way for a pauper to see  the world. His hobbies when not in port were always reading and writing. There were Short Story, Essay and Poetry competitions for British Seamen in those days which he usually managed win. This encouraged him to reach out a bit to magazines and such. Apart from the boost his ego wallowed, it supplied extra cash to explore foreign ports.

After having a (terrible) novel published the Merchant Navy brought him ashore to study. He got a B.Ed from London University and then began a desk job which didn't suit at all. He went back to sea and after the Falkland War found himself teaching in a High School in Turkey. Then he was teaching in the East End of London. (Teaching? Well, preventing mayhem anyway.)

Some years ago he moved to Central Portugal where he's earned a living by writing. Short stories are still his first love. He still has a lot more to learn though. Says Leo, "Sometimes, like today, I find that I have actually won, or been placed in 6 different competitions and I feel I can afford a little smugness. Then I read a winning story by 20 year old I've never heard of and think, That's brilliant! It's also humbling! I'm a sham. I might as well go back to sea. I was better at holystoning."

Which is a wonderful introduction to our second prize winner, **Diane Ward.** Miss Ward is a 17 year old aspiring writer from Brandon MS. Graduating high school early, she attended Belhaven university in 2009 on scholarship. She especially enjoys writing fantasy, science fiction, horror, and historical fiction.

Jack Noble is from Nairn in the north of Scotland. He currently lives in Guangzhou, China, where he teaches English. He has written a handful of stories over the years, and has always harboured an ambition to get his act together and get published. Suddenly realising he was thirty-five years old and still not a writer, he decided to make 2011 the year he became one. More recently he noticed he was thirty-six and still not a novelist. He plans to rectify this situation by the end of 2012.

Somer Brodribb was born in Canada and lives in England. Her story, 'The History Parrot,' was published by Cinnamon Press in 2009 and other stories were long-listed in 2007 and 2011. She has completed a novel and is writing another and more stories.

Christian Cook has published two novels, 'Broken Eggshells' (a black comedy about terrorism) and 'Pulling Power' (a dark medical tale). A third manuscript, 'Nix Ex Machina,' regarding online snow sales to the Inuit of Alaska, is nearing completion. When not writing, Christian is a freelance designer and photographer. He currently lives in Surrey, England, with his wife, two daughters and son.

Sharda Dean was born in the Caribbean, of Indian descent but has lived in or close to London for most of her life. She worked in the City as an economist in the 1990s but left to have her three children. She has also worked as a web designer, shop girl, and currently lives in the middle of a school. She has always enjoyed writing.

Jon Flieger is from Windsor. He is afraid of bees.

Suzanne Gaskell is married with two daughters and a step-son and have retired as a Senior Real Estate Sales Consultant. She lives in an urban multi-cultured suburb of Melbourne which she finds colourful and stimulating. Her husband and she have downsized to an apartment on the banks of the Maribrynong River and enjoy watching the changing patterns of river life. They spend as much time as money will allow on travel both overseas and interstate. She has been writing for approximately twelve months and has won a second place in verse and is currently shortlisted for a poem.

Vivian Hassan-Lambert's
writing has appeared in books,
magazines, net, radio and stage
including *Baby Magazine, BBC
Brazen Radio, Half-Empty
Bookcase, Jewish Chronicle,
Lillian Baylis Theatre, PulpNet,
QWF* and *TellTales 4 Anthology.*
She was short-listed for
Bridport 2010 and Serpents Tail
London Short Story award and
is a recipient of an Arts Council
Grants for the Art. She lives in
London with her husband and
daughter, but spent her

childhood in the warm air of Los Angeles. She is currently
working on a novel set in 1960s Los Angeles.

Sarah Hegarty lives in Guildford with her family. She aims to
write for 15 - 20 hours a week and has completed her first novel,
set in a future Britain reminiscent of 1970s China. She is inspired
by the work of David Mitchell and Margaret Atwood. She has a
Masters in Creative Writing from the University of Chichester.

Annie Mfula is a relative
newcomer to creative writing.
She started writing in early
2010 and draws on influences
from her native Zambia and
from her friends, neighbours
and life in sunny Surrey and

London. Annie enjoys the creativity of short fiction and horror stories and has had a short horror story published under her pen name Limerick A. Rainie. The story for "One Way Ticket to Mexico" was developed gradually and was inspired by a friend's toxic encounter with "the girlfriend of his dreams." Having the story picked for honourable mention and publication by Momaya has made Annie's year! Her plans for the future are to keep writing and to keep learning. She is currently working on a revision to her first children's fantasy novel.

Melanie Susan Marshall was born in Wiltshire in 1982. She completed an MA in Creative Writing at UEA. She currently works as a freelance editor and writer and lives in the south west of Englan with her husband and her two cats. Her favourite authors include Iris Murdoch and Jeremy Dyson.

Jennifer R Widrig teaches English in Seattle, Washington. Her poetry has been published in Crab Creek Review and The Bellowing Ark. She lives in Seattle with her husband and two children.

The Judges

Andy Callus is a newswire journalist who works as a copy editor for Reuters in London's Canary Wharf. He began his working life in 1980s Fleet Street, and has reported for Reuters and other newswires in Paris, Hong Kong, Singapore and Hanoi.

Kay Peddle was born in South Africa and moved to the UK in 2006. She has worked at a small South African literary press as a copy-editor, completed an MA in International Publishing at Oxford Brookes University, an internship at The World Bank and has done reading for a leading literary agency based in Oxford. She is currently an assistant editor at Random House.

Polly Courtney discovered her passion for writing in an unusual way: by starting a career as an investment banker. She was so shocked by what she found there that she quit her high-flying position to write a fictional expose on the square mile, based on her experiences. *Golden Handcuffs* came out in 2006 and since then, Polly has had five further titles published: *Poles Apart, The Day I Died, The Fame Factor, Defying Gravity* and *It's a Man's World.* Her novels have are all based on social issues or the stories of real people today. For more information, please visit www.pollycourtney.com

Alice Shepherd is currently an assistant editor at Penguin, where she works on a wide range of commercial fiction. Having started her publishing career at Abner Stein literary agency, she then went on to work at Headline Publishing Group.

Momaya Press

Monisha Saldanha earned her MBA at Harvard Business School in 2001 and has been working in publishing and internet commerce ever since. She believes that building a worldwide audience for the short story is vital to the promotion of this art form, and is proud that Momaya Press is increasingly recognized as the premiere forum for short story writers. She is currently finishing her first novel.

Maya Cointreau received a degree in Russian Literature from Smith College in 1996 and has over 15 years of experience in publishing and graphic arts. She has written and published five fiction and non-fiction books, and was managing editor of *DCC Magazine*, a magazine with a circulation of more than 60,000 readers. She works as an artist and graphic designer from her studio in Connecticut. Her writing and design work can be seen at foxravendesigns.com and mayacointreau.com.

.